MYTHICAL DESIRES UNIVERSE SHORT STORIES

M.L. EADEN

Print ISBN: 978-1-962655-08-8 – Douglas Illusions

eBook ISBN: 978-1-962655-07-1 – Douglas Illusions

Rare Temptations Book Cover by Joanne Kwan: https://linktr.ee/dashalutris

Xavior & Greg character art by Joanne Kwan

Rare Temptations character art by Clove: https://clvnhvs.carrd.co/

Vampire Trio & Merfolk family by Mara (Scales 'n' Art): https://linktr.ee/ningyo_gaaru

Other book covers by M.L. Eaden: https://mleaden.com/

1st edition 2023

Content Warnings: see each story for content warnings.

QUEER STORIES BASED IN MYTH, LEGEND, AND SCIENCE FICTION.

Reader's Note

The Universe you are entering is a contemporary one with magic, myths, and legends living and working alongside each other. There are many sentient and varied species. Some of them are out in the open while others are not. However, everyone knows they existed, knows there's magic in the world, and knows that whether something walks in the light or goes bump in the night, it's as real as the sunrise and sunset.

It's a world where science and magic work hand-in-hand, creating advanced technology and building a day-to-day life where you could easily meet a dragon astronaut, an orc mage specializing in medicine, or a fae working as a tailor. Moonbases exist, sustainable living is a reality, and promises which seem to be mere figments of imagination are woven into the fabric.

Enjoy!

TO DISCOVER MORE:

MLEADEN.COM/BOOKS

CONTENTS

Introduction   1

Prince's Tide   3

The Vampire Accords   31

The Saint George Chronicles   45

Firebaugh Resort   107

About The Resort   109

Miscellaneous   209

Important Events In History   232

About the Author   234

Also By M.L. Eaden   235

INTRODUCTION

Welcome to my collection of short stories all related to the Mythical Desires Universe. These have been written over the years from various ideas and projects, along with prompts provided by readers and promotional events. This will be the first time most of these stories will be published widely, and the first time they will be in print.

I'm very excited to share these with you and look forward to reader reactions. My hope is that this will be the first volume, with many more to come.

Enjoy!

M.L. Eaden

PRINCE'S TIDE

Prince's Tide

The Dinner Date

M.L. Eaden

AUTHOR'S NOTE
THE DINNER DATE

I wrote *Dinner Date* after the original Tapas run of *Prince's Tide* as an extra. I considered putting it into the book when it was published, but ultimately left it as an extra since it was a fairly lengthy story on its own and I couldn't decide where it fit in the book. However, I consider it to be part of canon and may answer a few things about how Royce stayed off the radar of paparazzi for so long.

Content Warnings: *on-page sex, stalking by paparazzi*

THE DINNER DATE

"So, what do you think? Is it a bad idea?"

Pete shrugged. "I think you'll have to at least give him a chance to dress up. You know how he was for your birthday. You take him to some fancy place like that, he'll be upset if he feels out of place."

Troller and I had been together for a while now, and I wanted to do something nice for him. Problem was, I wasn't sure what exactly. My birthday party was a pleasant surprise. Troller dressed up was even better.

"I got it!" I snapped my fingers and picked up my tablet. Made a few orders and a couple of reservations. One at a nice Italian place a friend of mine owned and the other at a nice hotel close to the port. "Could you let Marcy know I'm having a few things delivered to her shop?"

Pete chuckled. "That'll cost you."

"Whatever manual labor she has planned, she can double it. It will be worth the trouble."

Turns out, once Marcy knew what and who it was for, she didn't care. Troller was her favorite customer.

We made our usual stop at Marcy's bakery after docking and unloading our catch in the early hours. Kristy was the watch for the weekend while everyone else had plans onshore.

"Good morning, you three," Marcy said as Pete made a beeline for her. Troller and I followed him inside. She had two other folks working the counter that morning, so she could step away. Saturdays were always busy, and we were often roped into maintenance projects that had piled up during the weeks we were out on the water.

Troller and I watched as Pete kissed Marcy and wrapped his arms around her. "You smell," she said playfully as she scrunched her nose.

"That's the smell of hard work, babe," Pete said.

"Well, if you don't go upstairs and clean up, you'll be hard up later," replied Marcy.

"Aye, captain," Pete said softly as he kissed her cheek, and Marcy moved away from him to grab a box off the counter.

"Here, take this with you and take these two upstairs," she said as she handed Pete a pastry box and pointed at Troller and me. "Give Royce the packages next to the door."

"Sure thing, al te quiero," Pete said as he leaned in for a quick kiss before leaving Marcy to her customers.

"Yo también te quiero!" Marcy replied. "Nice to see you two again." She waved.

"Thank you for the pastries, Marcy!" Troller called back as we followed Pete upstairs to their apartment.

Once upstairs, Pete handed me packages and the box of pastries. "I'll let you two figure out where you'll land next, but you'll excuse me if I kick you out. I need to clean up because Marcy has plans." Troller and I snickered like school kids, but Pete didn't crack a joke. On the contrary, he was all business, as he politely shoved us out the rear apartment door that led to a porch above the alleyway.

Once the door closed, Troller smiled, glancing between the door and me. "If I were separated from my mate and were only able to see them at certain times, I'd forgo any other companionship until I was properly reunited." He fished out a danish and took a bite as we walked down the back stairs.

I chuckled. "Yeah, I suppose we have an advantage. I'm able to see you every night after work."

"Among other things," Troller said as he stopped a few steps behind me. I turned around as he leaned toward me. We shared some sweet kisses until Troller got curious. "What's in the box-es, Royce?"

"You'll see. But first, I have a surprise." I had a vehicle service pick us up at Marcy's and take us to the hotel I booked for the weekend. When we arrived in the corner suite, I dropped our bag, the boxes, and Troller abandoned the pastries for the view.

"Royce, it's magical. You can see the whole port from here."

"I'm glad you like it." I found the bottle of bubbly I ordered waiting in an iced pail just inside the door. Troller turned around as I popped the cork. I picked up two glasses from the nearby desk and poured one for each of us. I put the bottle back and handed one glass to Troller. "To our first weekend getaway."

He held the glass as if it was the most fragile thing in the world. I tapped mine against his, and he blushed and laughed at the noise.

"Royce, how does it make bubbles?"

"Oh! That's carbonation and fermentation. When you pour it out, it reacts with the air and causes bubbles." He watched me sip my glass and smiled. Then he took a tiny sip.

"That's nice. I like bubbles." And then the rest of it went down the hatch as I blinked. "Can I have more?"

"Uh, sure. But you'll want to take this one slower, I think."

"I've had beer on the boat. This tastes better."

I'd only ever seen Troller drink beer a few times, and he didn't really like it, but it was something the crew did together. "I'm glad you like it." As I refilled his glass, I called out to the au tomated system. "Lights at twenty-five percent, and play some soft classical music, please."

The room adjusted, and Troller smiled as I scooped him into my arms.

"Did you plan on us leaving the room?"

"No, not for a while. Is that alright?"

"It's perfect."

I kissed Troller as we danced a little longer. By the end of our second glass, we were reaching for each other's clothes. Troller's legs led us toward the bed before I stopped us and pointed us to the bathroom. Once I'd danced us inside the room, he saw the large tub.

"Royce! What's this?"

"A jacuzzi. It fills with water and has jets that make bubbles." He looked excited as I gave him another kiss. "Here, let me start it up." Fifteen minutes later, we were naked and sitting in a sizable two-person tub full of warm, bubbling water.

Troller played with the bubbles, and I watched as we relaxed. There wasn't anywhere to be, at least not until later tonight. "What are you thinking?"

"It's odd to be in this much water and not swim. Plus, the warmth and bubbles are new. Much different from the water closet on the boat."

"True," I said, then reached for his hand. "I wanted you to try something different, but if it bothers you, we can use the shower."

"No," he shook his head as he moved toward me. "I like it. But then again, I like anywhere you are, Royce."

"Ah, so that's the real reason."

He smiled as he moved and settled onto my lap. "It's a good reason."

"I won't disagree with that." I picked up a sponge and soaked it with water, then squeezed it over Troller's shoulder. He plucked it out of my hand the second he noticed.

"This is much softer than I expected! We use something like this to help remove dead scales."

"Works the same here, but we use it to remove dead skin. Turn around, and I'll wash your back." I took my time using the sponge over the expanse of his back. Tracing his strong shoulders and muscles, he developed from swimming and working on the boat.

"That feels wonderful, my love," Troller said with a sigh.

I continued with his arms and shoulders, then pulled him closer to me and worked the sponge across his chest and abdomen. Troller was utterly relaxed, but for one part of his body that lay erect along his stomach. I was in a similar state of excitement, but liked the view more than anything. As he floated, I eased his hair loose and let the long strands of red flow across my body.

We stayed in the water until we both had wrinkled skin. Once we extracted ourselves from the tub, Troller went to the shower to wash his hair. Wrapped up in fluffy hotel towels, we crawled into the enormous bed for a nap. I set an alarm so we could wake up in time for my other surprises.

TROLLER

Royce's alarm beeped softly, and I reached over to shut it off. He sighed as I rubbed myself along his stout body. The sigh turned into a soft groan that gave me other ideas as the towel wrapped around his waist fell open.

"Love." I kissed his chest and nipped at it lightly. "Are you awake?" The 'hmmm' in response amused me until I licked his nipple.

"I am now. Hello there. Have a good nap?" I could tell he was smiling by the shape of his beard. It amused me to no end that his facial hair framed his facial features.

I nodded, then continued my journey down his chest and across his abdomen as he sighed softly. He was half-hard when I reached for his shaft. The soft groan turned into a moan of pleasure, which sent tingles down my spine. The slow-motion of my hand caused Royce to flex his hips in a lazy effort to chase the sensation. "Would you like more?"

"Mmm, yes," Royce moaned. I increased my strokes, and as I was about to bring the crown of his cock into my mouth, he yelled out. "No, wait, wait. Let me check the time."

"What for?" His response surprised me. Royce only ever turned down sex during working hours, which was fair. Teasing each other until we were off the clock was a fun game we liked to play, but there was no work here.

Royce checked his cell phone. I felt slightly annoyed at his lack of an answer. "You're ruining the mood, my love."

"Sorry, love, I only want to make sure we have enough time." He put his phone down, making me curious.

"Time for sex?"

"Well, yes, but no. We should start getting ready." He gently pushed me away, frustrating me more.

"What? Why?"

He sat up and gave me a grin, clever eyes taking their fill of my half-dressed form. "You'll see. But first. I want to give you something." Royce hopped out of bed, naked, and I was almost ready to forgive him just for the view alone as he bent over to grab the packages he'd left by the door.

When he came back, he handed me one and held onto the other. I tore at the paper wrapping and opened the box. Inside was a mess of sequins. When I extracted it from the box, it unfurled into a stylish pantsuit. The blouse was completely sheer lace, and the pants were covered in sequins. A suit jacket followed that matched the pants.

I was so in awe of the garment that I almost missed what Royce said. "Troller, you don't have time."

"What?"

"There's a salon downstairs. I made an appointment for you. They can fix your hair however you'd like."

"Why won't you fix it for me? You're good at it."

"I'm alright, but they are much better. Trust me." He gave me a quick kiss. "If you don't like it, then we won't do it again."

I didn't know what Royce was planning, but I didn't like the idea of leaving the room without him. I'd rather go back to my previous idea of having sex in a bed bigger than our room on the boat. "Royce, what's this all about?"

"My surprise." He stood and purposefully kept the box he held in front of him as he leaned down to give me another kiss.

"What's in the box?" I pointed at it, and instead, Royce turned and sauntered toward the bathroom. The sight distracted me, and I almost didn't hear his reply.

"You'll see. Now go before you're late." With that, Royce disappeared into the bathroom and shut the door.

I looked down at my box and noticed another item. Black lace panties. Well, at least I knew where the night would end up, whatever surprise Royce had in mind. I put everything back in the box and headed out the door wearing my robe. Once I was in the lobby, I asked where the "salon" was located. They showed me into a large room with windows. Inside, there were chairs and several individuals moving about, arranging hair into various styles. I had read about a place like this, but hadn't visited one. Land dwellers had developed some interesting skills.

Inside the salon, they quickly guided me to a chair where several individuals near me seemed fascinated with my hair.

"Sweetheart, it's beautiful," one of them said.

"So long," said another.

"It's in wonderful condition, too. How do you maintain it?" A third person looked at me with envy.

"I eat plenty of fish." I said. They laughed, and I smiled as one of them took up a position behind the chair I occupied.

"I'll have to up my intake then. But seriously, do you have any idea what you'd like to do with your hair?" asked the person standing behind me. They were slightly older and had pretty brown hair cut short that looked like it wouldn't move in a strong wind. I even doubted it would move underwater. They gently touched my scalp, then began combing my hair.

"I usually braid it. Or Royce does."

"Oh, hmm, okay. Maybe we should try something a teeny bit different," they said, while holding their thumb and forefinger a centimeter apart. "What do you say?"

"Okay." I nodded, and the hairdresser went into action. They used many potions until my hair shined, then they snipped a few pieces here and there, but not too much. As they dried my hair, the hairdresser used another tool they called a curling wand. It made curls in my hair with a flick of the wrist.

The curls were pretty. I wondered as I watched my hair turn into layers of curls if Royce could help me purchase such a device. However, the lack of practicality became clear. Before long, I had three people working with wands to curl my hair. "Is this taking too long?"

"Nope, you're fine. Your date said to have you ready by eight o'clock. We still have an entire hour. You'll have plenty of time to change, even."

Whatever Royce had planned was elaborate. By seven-thirty, my hair had been pinned up and spiraled like coral. There was no way it would last the night. But I hoped it would stay put until Royce saw it. The salon let me change into my outfit in one of their restrooms. When I had the panties and the pantsuit on, I picked up the jacket and noticed a pair of gray and black shoes. They wrapped my feet in protective comfort, as if I were wearing no shoes at all. I slipped the jacket on, careful of my hair, and admired myself in the full-length mirror. Royce had done very well selecting my outfit. The shimmer of the jacket and pants was mesmerizing, and the sheer blouse highlighted the muscles of my chest. A feature Royce often professed to enjoy touching.

I slipped my hands into the jacket pockets and felt a piece of paper in the one on the right. It was a small card, and when I pulled it out, it read—Meet me in the lobby—Royce.

As I exited the restroom, there were sudden gasps and notes of surprise. "What? Did I mess up my hair?"

"No, lovely, it's perfect. You're perfect. But give me two minutes to make it better, please?" The hairdresser held their hands in front of their face as if they were worshiping something. Maybe it was a deity of hair. Their earnest face made me give in to their request.

I nodded. "Alright."

They swooped in and led me back to a chair. Once seated, they began by applying something to my eyes. I watched, fascinated by this. Once they were done with my eyes, they picked up another tube.

"Pucker your lips. Like this," they said, demonstrating what looked like an exaggerated kiss. I did as requested, and they applied a tinted salve to my lips, rendering them a dark, sparkling red that nearly matched my hair. The eye paint made my lashes darker and gave me dark swoops on either side of my eyes. "It's called cat eye makeup. It really makes your irises pop, don't you think?"

The paint did highlight my black irises. I hoped Royce recognized me. I barely recognized myself in the large mirror.

"Go on, sweetie. Hurry, or you'll be late," they said, as they gave me a nudge out of the chair.

I smiled as I stood and then turned toward the door. I stopped a few steps away, realizing I hadn't thanked them for their work, or paid, and turned back to the wonderful person who had helped me. "Thank you for your exceptional work. Do you need compensation?"

They smiled. "No, sweetie, your date took care of everything."

"That doesn't surprise me. He's thoughtful." I turned to leave, then turned back. "May I have your name so I can request your services again?"

"It's Baylee, sweetheart. Or Bay. What's yours?"

"Troller."

"Well, that's certainly unique." They smiled and came toward me, gently put their hands on my shoulders and turned me toward the door, whispering. "Knock them dead, sweetie."

"Thank you, Baylee!" I waved as I left and quickly went to the lobby, though I had no idea what his sentiment meant. I certainly didn't want Royce dead.

The lobby was full of people. Some of them dressed formally, and others came in like Royce and I had earlier, exhausted and wearing comfortable clothes. Not that what I wore wasn't comfortable. It was. The pants of the suit swished like a skirt, but longer. I was so enamored by it I almost missed Royce.

He had his back to me, but I would recognize his shoulders anywhere. The jacket and black pants he wore accentuated all of his features. When he turned, he buttoned up his jacket and smiled at me. He even wore a funny length of black ribbon around his neck, tied into a bow. I grinned at him, picking up my pace.

The distance between us vanished, and it seemed as if we were the only ones standing in the lobby. "You look wonderful, Royce."

"You, my love, my Troller, look ravishing." We kissed softly, and then Royce stepped back and offered his arm. I threaded mine through his as he led the way out of the hotel. A stylish vehicle with a person holding the door open smiled at us.

"Good evening, Your Highness," said the person holding the door. As we exited, there was a buzz and a flash.

I blinked like a dazed fish. "Royce, what happened?"

"Someone's taking pictures." He looked at the person holding the door with a grimace as he helped me into the vehicle and then followed.

As the vehicle drove off, I panicked. "Royce! There isn't anyone driving!!"

"It's alright. It's programmed and knows where to go." A piece of soft music played, and Royce settled on the seat next to me as he unbuttoned his jacket.

The windows were tinted, and it was already late in the evening, which made it hard to see any of the city, but what I saw was beautiful. I turned to Royce to say as much, but his face had a strained look about it. "What's wrong?"

"I wanted everything to be perfect," he said with a sigh. "I followed all the protocols. I thought we'd have one weekend to ourselves."

"Are you worried about the pictures?" He nodded. "They're just pictures, love. They won't ruin our night."

"What if they find out who you are?" He frowned, obviously concerned.

I shrugged. "Then they do. Because all they would find out is that I'm with you." I reached for his hand and threaded our fingers together. "Whatever you planned will be wonderful because we're together."

He relaxed slightly. "I hope so."

I smiled, then ventured to ask, "Where are we going?"

He finally cracked a small smile. "Well, it's one of my favorite places to eat. So I wanted to share it with you."

"Then I look forward to this place. How much farther is it?" Instead of Royce answering, the vehicle did.

"Your destination is approximately twenty-five minutes away, passenger."

"Royce," I captured his attention from the window.

"Hmm?"

I leaned toward him and gently put my lips to his. He responded then, kissing me back with interest. His large hands slipped into my jacket, and their warmth as they slid along my chest and sides generated an internal warmth that made my heart ache with need. I crawled into his lap and barely missed the roof of the vehicle as we continued to kiss. His beard rasped along my skin and made me gasp into his mouth as our tongues teased and licked.

"I love you so much, Troller. So much." Royce babbled.

While Royce's hands caressed my body, the only part of him that wasn't clothed was his face. It was frustrating. I reached between us and rubbed his obvious hard-on. "I want you, love. Please."

The vehicle's voice interrupted us. "We will reach your destination in five minutes."

The annoyed groan I made had Royce chuckling. "Don't worry, love. We'll have time enough later. I promise." I whimpered in frustration.

The vehicle slowed and rounded a corner. I moved from Royce's lap, if only to exit the motorized annoyance. The building our vehicle pulled up to was understated but nice. The name on the sign above the door read "De Luca's."

Royce opened the door, and an individual in uniform greeted us. "Welcome, friends, to De Luca's." They escorted us to the door, and as it opened, another individual greeted Royce.

"My friend! I'm delighted you contacted me. I have your table ready." They saw me and smiled, then placed a hand on Royce's shoulder. A fit of jealousy shot through me. Why was he so familiar with Royce? "Royce," he said in a soft voice. "Who is this lovely individual you've brought with you tonight?"

"Marco, this is Troller."

Marco glanced between us and then offered his hand to me. I took it, and he glanced up at me as he turned my hand and placed another on top of mine. "Enchanted." He smiled again, then let go. "Please, my friends, follow me."

We had a private table in a small space near the kitchen area with a potted plant in the center. That caught my attention. It meant I wouldn't have to smell decay while we ate. It must have been Royce's suggestion, given the vases of flowers I saw on the other tables we passed. Marco seated us both, and as we removed our jackets, another individual came to retrieve them from Marco's hands.

"My friends, tonight we have a lovely '85 Malbec that I've opened for your arrival. My chef has worked her special magic, and you'll be treated to an exceptional menu that I am very sure will delight your senses and fill your stomach." Marco poured the wine into the waiting glasses. "Enjoy. Please press the button under the corner of the table if you need anything."

"Thank you, Marco." Marco touched Royce's shoulder again, and Royce patted his hand as he left. He smirked at me, likely picking up on my mood. "Your eyes are narrowed in the same way you look at Pete sometimes when we joke around. With the makeup, it makes you look rather dangerous, love." Royce picked up his glass and took a sip. I didn't touch mine.

"Do you know him intimately?" I whispered.

"Who, Marco?" he asked. I nodded. "It was a very long time ago. We're friends now."

"Oh? Does he know that?"

"You're jealous?"

"I am. He places his hands on you as if he has permission." Royce blinked as his eyes grew wide. I took a deep breath and sighed.

"Troller, that's how Marco shows his friendship, and how he expresses himself. Also, he has permission to touch me like that. We've known each other for a very long time. It's the same as Pete giving me a hug or a pat on the back."

That soothed the sting a bit, but only so much. I had friends too, whom I hugged and touched. It was not uncommon, nor was it unique, to be intimate with friends. "I'm sorry, my love. Maybe it's all the newness causing me to behave poorly."

Royce reached his hand out toward me. I took it. "I know you trust me, but maybe I should have explained more than I did about my surprise this evening. You've been very patient with me."

I squeezed his hand. "And you've obviously done a lot of planning. I do not mean to be ungrateful."

"You're not; never think that." Royce raised my hand to his lips and kissed it. "So, let me explain. Tonight, you are being treated to fresh, authentic Italian fare. Six courses total, which includes all the bread you can eat." As if the word were magic itself, the smell of fresh bread wafted into the room, followed by a server who placed a basket on the table, bursting full of all kinds of bread. They explained all the fresh breads, then talked about the salted butter and tomato jam that would best go with which one. When they left, I was so delighted that it was hard to choose which one to start with.

"Here, let me help you." Royce took a round loaf from the basket and broke off some and handed it to me. I took a bite and moaned. His chuckle broke my reverence. "Marcy isn't the only one who knows how to make bread."

"No, she isn't, apparently. But I'm not going to tell her that, are you?" I asked.

"No," Royce said with a grin on his face.

The rest of dinner whirled by with one dish after another, much of it featuring fish or some kind of sea life so fresh that there was no hint of decay whatsoever. All of it was amazing, but nothing compared to what they offered for dessert.

"For my two favorite patrons, our very best," Marco said. "I'm told," Marco looked at me as he set the dish in front of both of us, "that you are a connoisseur of pastries. Is that correct?"

I smiled at Royce, then at Marco. "That's correct."

"Well then, our famous tiramisu might delight you." Marco smiled at me, then picked up what Royce had called a dessert fork from the table and offered it to me. "Please let me know what you think." I took the fork from his hand while I looked at Royce. It seemed everyone was eager for my opinion of this confection. I cut through a corner of the dessert and immediately noticed the layers of cream and some kind of bread. When I put the bite in my mouth, I couldn't make a sound for the flavors that spread across my tongue.

"I think you have a winner, Marco." Royce's voice made me glance up from my plate. I hadn't noticed I'd nearly finished the dessert without a word and nodded as they both laughed.

"Excellent! Excellent!" Marco smiled at me. "Would you like another?"

"Yes, please." We all laughed. As Marco waved to the server to bring another, I could admit, I might have overreacted earlier.

When we were done, Marco returned with our jackets and helped us into them. "I want to thank both of you for allowing me to entertain your senses this evening. Please do not hesitate to return when you can. I would love nothing more than to entertain you both again."

Marco shook Royce's hand, then turned and offered his to me. I took it, and he turned my hand over and glanced at me. "May I, my darling?" I nodded, and he placed the smallest of kisses on my skin.

"Okay, that's enough, you charmer," Royce said as he tapped his friend's shoulder.

"I can't help myself. You have a most handsome partner, my friend. I'm quite envious of you."

One of the servers from earlier in the evening entered the room, went to Marco, and whispered into his ear. "Whoever told them will be scrubbing floors with a toothbrush. Call my private service and have them bring my vehicle to the back."

"What's happened?" Royce looked at his friend, concerned.

"Someone has told the gawkers you're here. Many imagers are hovering outside of the front door, just above the sign. One of my employees noticed when they were on the roof for a break."

Royce sighed. "That means they probably know the hotel we are staying at as well."

Marco waved his hand. "Do not worry, Royce. I'll have my service take you to the hotel's private entrance. You're staying at the Grand, yes?" Royce nodded. "Ah, a creature of habit." He patted Royce on the shoulder again. "It's a lovely place, but you might pick somewhere else next time."

"I used discretion. I don't know how the media found me."

"The determined will always find their prey." Marco glanced at me. "Isn't that right, Troller?"

I wondered then how much Royce had told his friend. I smiled because I knew Marco was a tiny bit more than envious. "Yes, it is."

Marco's vehicle was older but nearly as nice as the one we'd arrived in. As Royce helped me into the vehicle, he smiled, then turned to Marco and gave him a hug. "Thank you for everything tonight."

"Yes, thank you, Marco," I said as I poked my head out.

"Be safe, the both of you." Royce got into the vehicle, and Marco closed the door and tapped the roof. This time, there was a driver, and they lowered a piece of glass that separated our seats from theirs.

"I'll have you back at the hotel safe and sound within twenty minutes. Their security has been alerted and knows we'll be there shortly," said the driver.

"Thank you." Royce didn't look happy about all the fuss. It was undoubtedly more complicated than our usual weekends on the boat.

"Hey." My voice drew his gaze to mine. "You shouldn't make that face."

"Oh? Why not?" Royce frowned. I leaned toward him and pressed my lips to his ear.

"Because I'm about to have you under me for the rest of the evening, and I can't imagine a better way to spend a night with you." I felt the skin of Royce's ear flush with heat against my lips as his breath hitched.

The rest of the ride to the hotel was filled with silent anticipation. Security took us to our room, and once delivered to the door, Royce thumbed it open and let me inside. The moment he closed the door, I was on him.

"Oof. Troller. Shit." He grabbed my ass and lifted me. I wrapped my legs around his waist as he walked us to the bed. I shoved his jacket off his wide frame as he pulled at mine. Our lips never stopped as we tangled tongues. When Royce reached the bed, I slid down him until my ass hit the mattress.

Royce pulled at the ribbon around his neck and the buttons of his shirt as I worked at his belt and zipper. He was barely done with half his buttons when I pulled his hard length free. I shoved him into my mouth and moaned around him. It's all I had thought about once we were alone. His fingers tangled into my hair and gently pulled out pins that let my soft tresses fall to my shoulders.

"Fuck, Troller. Don't stop."

We were still wearing too many clothes, but I didn't care in my determination to touch him. My hands drifted from Royce's dick to his ass. I groped at the firm globes of flesh and pushed his trousers down to the floor. His fingers fisted in my hair, and I knew he was close. My tongue danced over his swollen flesh as I massaged his backside. My name on his lips was my second warning. I brought a hand back to his front and cupped his balls. He nearly doubled over when he came with a loud grunt. I held him up until he caught his breath, then I eased us onto the bed together.

"That was amazing," Royce said as he lay there dazed while I helped him out of the rest of his clothes. He was gloriously naked under me, and I ran my hands through the dark hair that covered his body.

"You're not passing out on me, are you?"

"I wouldn't dream of it."

I patted his chest and went to retrieve our lube out of the bag we had brought with us. Royce sat up and watched me walk back toward the bed.

"Can I undress you?" I nodded as I tossed the bottle on the bed. Royce stood and moved behind me. As rough as I had been with him, he was gentle. His hands glided down my back and into the garment, first to feel up my ass, then to rub my cock. I groaned as his hand cupped me and promised more. He left me panting as his hands moved on to help me strip.

Once I was only in my panties, his hands found my hips and pulled me back against him. Royce caressed my body as his lips pressed kisses along my neck and shoulders. "That feels wonderful, Royce."

"Mmm hmm." His hand caressed me through the panties, then pushed them aside to take my length in his hand. I stood still as he stroked me gently. I hadn't noticed when Royce had prompted me to bend over the bed in my present state of bliss. When my face pressed against the mattress, I smiled, expecting what might come next. I picked up the lube at my side and held it up as a silent offering.

I couldn't have been more wrong about what Royce planned as he let go of my cock, put both hands on my asscheeks, gently spreading them. A moment later, his moist tongue licked my hole. I dropped the bottle and fisted the bedclothes in an attempt to stay in one place and push my ass further into Royce's face. Royce licked the scant fabric of my panties, then pushed it aside with his tongue and licked me again until it slipped back into place.

The noises I made reminded me of the kinds of clicks and whistles we'd use along the currents to pass messages at long distances. I was not the least quiet and had wholly forgotten any surface dweller language.

Royce eventually gave up playing with the panties and pushed them down my thighs as he continued to lick and probe me with his tongue. Then he did something with his tongue and stroked my cock in such a way that I came as a high-pitched wail passed my lips while my face was pressed into the mattress.

Even as my drool made a pool under me, I used what sense I had left to speak. "More, Royce. Fuck me. Please."

His low chuckle vibrated through me as he kissed one ass cheek, then the other. I heard the lube bottle open and felt the cool liquid slide down my crease. With Royce's loving attention, I relaxed for him. As the head of his cock pushed further into me, I moaned softly. He moved slowly at first, applying more lube as he pulled out, then pushed back into me.

I knew from experience that while Royce could recover quickly, the second time took longer than the first. I usually came before he did, if only because his cock would rub against a spot that could only be reached in my human form.

"Royce, Royce, my love."

"Hmmm?"

"Come, lie down." I had to repeat myself before he finally stopped and lay next to me on the bed. I crawled over him and positioned myself above him. His hands went to my ass and held me in place while I positioned his dick.

The slow slide back onto Royce's cock had him groaning as he watched. My hair bounced around my shoulders as I drew myself up and thrust myself back down. The dark hair that covered his body was laced with his sweat. I bent over to lick his chest and taste the salt of him.

He chuckled until I nipped at him. "Ah!" We laughed as I continued to fuck him. I leaned back, and he reached for my softened cock. "Fuck, you're beautiful, love." He said between pants. "So gorgeous and handsome." He sucked in another breath. "I'm so lucky to have your love. My life feels fulfilled because of you, Troller."

Royce always said sweet things in bed, but this was exceptional. "You are my heart," I said as I leaned forward again and kissed him. We thrust at each other until we both were covered in sweat and cum.

Afterward, I lay on Royce's chest as he played with my hair. "Did you enjoy today?" he asked.

"Yes, my love. It was one of the best days we've spent together."

"Even with the interruptions?"

"It made it more interesting," I said as I played with his chest hair. "I do not envy your parents, and can only imagine what they deal with every day." I lifted my head to look at him. "It makes more sense to me why you prefer to stay on the boat."

"When I planned this, I had nearly forgotten how difficult it was to move around sometimes."

"Don't be too hard on yourself. Everything turned out all right in the end." I pressed a kiss onto his chest and sighed.

"You're right." He bent to kiss my head. "Would you like to clean up?"

"Yes, soon." Soon never came as we both dozed off until Royce's phone woke us up the following morning.

ROYCE

A soft ring woke me up. Troller was still in my arms, but the phone was insistent. When I saw who it was, I answered. "Hello?"

"You've caused quite a stir, son. Are you and Troller alright?"

"What do you mean?"

"There are some fetching pictures of you splashed all over the web this morning. Troller too, but the media hasn't figured out who he is yet. Only that the two of you look rather elegant together."

I sighed. It had to be the pictures they took last night when we left the hotel. "I'm sorry, Pop." Ben, as always, was concerned about my welfare.

"No need to be sorry. We'll have to work up a different identification for you. Apparently, the media caught on to this one."

"Marco said as much."

"Ah, Marco. I miss his linguine," Ben said.

"Pop." My parents liked Marco. His cooking certainly helped. But Marco had never liked my job, and I wasn't willing to leave my boat. Leo understood. Ben didn't and had often asked about him—and Pete, too, come to think of it. Thankfully, Marco had. He would have done the same if someone had asked him to leave his restaurant behind. We remained friends even after the breakup. My parents still asked him to cater their events from time to time if they were anywhere near Texas.

"I meant no offense. Troller is an amazing chap, too. The pictures are stunning, I must say." I waited Ben out, not offering details as to why we were out in the city last night. "Let me know when you both want to return to your boat. I'll have a roof transport standing by to take you."

Troller put his hand on my arm, and I smiled down at him. "Tell them I said hello."

"Troller says to tell you both hi."

"Give him our love. I'll try to keep Papa from worrying when he wakes up."

Even when they had removed Ben from his post, he hadn't withdrawn from protecting Leo or me. It was his life's work. "We'll let you know when to send the transport. Let Papa know he can call later if he wants to."

"Alright, son. Love you. Stay safe."

"Love you too, Pop." I ended the call and looked at Troller. In the soft morning light, his hair was a crimson fire dashed across his pillow. I put down my phone and curled back up with him, wrapping my arms around his shoulders.

"Is everything alright?" he asked.

"Apparently, the hotel lobby and the building are being watched by the media. So Leo and Ben are sending a roof transport later to take us back to the port."

"That's nice of them."

"They know how much the spotlight is not my thing. Plus, I want to keep you safe. The less the media knows about you, the better."

Troller nodded. His makeup hadn't smudged, so when he blinked and stretched, I amused myself with the idea that I was sleeping next to an enormous cat instead of an individual that could live in the ocean. He smiled at me, and I brushed a lock of his hair behind his ear.

"What were you thinking just now?" he asked.

"That it's early, and we have a few more hours before we have to check out."

"Mmm hmm." Troller leaned into me and pressed his lips to mine. "I might have a few ideas."

"I thought you might."

When we made it back to the boat via air transportation provided by my parents. Pete had a grin on his face when we boarded the boat.

"What's got you smiling?" I asked.

"We let you off the boat for one night, and you two caused a sensation along the entire Gulf." Pete handed me a small box. "Thought you should have one memento of the evening. I'm assuming the two of you didn't think to take pictures."

I opened the box, and inside was one of the photographs floating around on the web, framed. Most of the ones the media latched onto either showed my anger or Troller looking surprised. This one was unique because it showed Troller and me looking at each other with affection written across our faces. "Thanks, Pete."

Pete shrugged. "It's too bad they were so obsessed about you turning up instead of realizing the two of you were happy."

I handed Troller the picture Pete had framed for us. "This is lovely. Thank you, Pete." The fascination on Troller's face stayed there for some time. I don't know if it was because of the picture or maybe he saw the same affection and love I'd seen in the photo.

"You're both welcome," Pete said.

I patted Pete on the back as we moved inside. "You'd think I was a unicorn returned from their dimension or something the way the media acts sometimes." Pete chuckled and nodded his agreement.

In the hallway, Troller gave me a quick kiss. "I know exactly where to put this." He turned toward our room with the photo and our bag in hand.

I went to the nest and checked the boat to ensure it was ready to leave in the morning. "Has everyone checked back in yet?"

"Yep, all present and accounted for, Captain," Pete said.

I nodded. "Good. I'll be happy to head back out. I have a good feeling about this week."

Little did I know our lives were about to change beyond anything I could imagine.

M.L. Eaden
Scales n Art

THE VAMPIRE ACCORDS

Author's Note
Midnight Lounge

I originally planned *Midnight Lounge* as part of the second book in the Vampire Accords trilogy. During successive rewrites, I discovered that the chapter really didn't work for the story, but I really liked the fact that Mason, Ian, and Jason had found their way to Firebaugh Resort. I also shared this short story in my newsletter as a NSFW bonus. This is the first time I have published it to a larger audience.

Content Warnings: *on-page sex, infection risk*

MIDNIGHT LOUNGE

Firebaugh Resort, December

MASON

"Who's idea was this again?" Ian asked as he, Jason, and I were all being massaged in the same room by three very skilled massage therapists.

"Mine. You're welcome," I said as Chuck, a tall bluish-green orc with large hands and a friendly smile, worked over my back and hips like I was play-dough.

A well-placed thumb made me gasp with pain, interrupting my scattered thoughts before I relaxed again. "You're very tense for someone that's mostly dead," Chuck said as he attacked my thighs and gluteal muscles, his large hands making quick work of the knots there.

"That's their fault." I quipped. There was a collective exasperation in the bond, which made me laugh. "Okay, it's mostly my fault. But it's not like I go looking for it." Ian made a noise of disbelief. I don't blame him. I didn't really believe what I was saying, either. "Only sometimes."

Chuck laughed. "It's nice to be loved."

"Yes. I agree. Most of the time." The guys laughed, and I sighed as Chuck continued his work.

"How's the pressure?" Chuck dug into my muscles.

"Good, very good."

When Chuck finished, he pulled the sheet over my back, using it to absorb the excess massage oil. "Try not to undo all my work by getting into trouble while you're here."

"Just gives me a reason to come back," I said as I lifted myself up to smile at him.

He smiled back and left with the other therapists. Jason, Ian and I sat up so we could pull on our robes.

"You are such a flirt, Mason," Jason said as he tied his robe.

"So are you. I heard your masseuse giggling," Ian said with an accent that sounded more posh than usual.

"I made a joke, and she laughed. That's not my fault." Jason gave us a shrug that didn't match his delighted smile.

I laughed. "We're all horrible flirts, and that's perfectly fine." The guys came over and wrapped me in their arms, and I snuggled into their artificial warmth. "Speaking of which, what do we want to do with the rest of our night?"

"It's a little past midnight. The lounge should be open," Jason said.

The Midnight Lounge was a club geared toward vampires visiting Firebaugh resort. Though since the incident at the resort a few years ago, they didn't get as many vampire visitors as they used to.

We cleaned up from our massages and put on casual clothes for the night. I wore my usual jeans and a t-shirt, while Ian was in dark slacks and a gray button-down, and Jason wore dark jeans and a light pink button-down with the sleeves rolled up. Jason and I kept Ian between us as we found a spot in the club to order drinks and people-watch.

There were a mix of patrons, some human-seeming who were probably shifters or mages. A few others were your typical nightlife folks. Nocturnal types like goblins, trolls, and vampires. Usually, if you saw them in more public settings, they used glamours to change their appearance. But here, things were relaxed; we were relaxed. It made for a friendly vibe.

After our first round of drinks, Jason stood and held out his hands. "Let's dance."

Ian and I shared a glance, then smiled and followed Jason's lead.

Of the three of us, Jason was the better dancer. Ian was very good at following, and I was good at getting caught up around someone's arms or feet. Dancing with someone else was never my strong suit unless the music was slow, and the steps were pretty basic. After a few turns on the dance floor, I let Jason and Ian dance while I found a place to watch.

An orc came up to my table and set down his drink. "Staying out of trouble?" he asked. I looked up and realized it was Chuck.

"Mostly. What about you?" Chuck was dressed in board shorts and a nice short-sleeved button-up that showed off his arms. The look was much more casual than the spa scrubs I'd seen him in earlier.

He shrugged. "If I were, I wouldn't be here talking with you."

"Oh yeah? What makes you say that?" I wondered if there was a policy about fraternizing with guests. But if Chuck was off the clock, which seemed to be the case, mingling with guests shouldn't be too much of a problem. Though he had called me trouble, so maybe he wanted to do more than talk.

He leaned down slightly and smiled. His dark amber eyes glinted in the low light. "You put me in the mind to break some rules."

I grinned. "How many rules are you breaking right now?"

"None. Yet. We're just talking." He nodded to the guys on the dance floor. "What about them?"

I glanced at them. They knew who I was talking to. They were talking about it; I could tell that much. Would they be interested? I conveyed that thought through our bond, and there was definitely an interest.

"Well, that would depend. Were you looking for something solo, or a group activity?"

Chuck glanced at them and smiled. "I'd never turn down more participants."

And that's how we ended up with my masseuse in our hotel suite. We had another round of drinks, though Chuck stuck to water.

The conversation stayed to safe topics until Jason pushed it. "So tell us, mate, do you want to kiss her?" My gaze bounced from Jason to Chuck and back. Chuck smiled and held out his large hand. I took it, and he pulled me onto his lap. His tusks framed my face, and his lips were soft when he pressed them to mine. My hand drifted to his short buzz cut hair as his hands moved to my hips.

I heard kissing behind us and knew Jason and Ian were engaged in a similar activity. Chuck's hand drifted up from my hip to under my shirt. It was large enough to cover half my torso, and I'm not small by human standards. I hadn't noticed that while he was massaging me. It made me realize how much his touch had relaxed me earlier. This time, it stoked my libido into a high flame. He kissed me again as I reached for my shirt. Then stopped me for a moment before I took it off. "If you need to stop, tell me what your safe word is, so I know."

My eyes went wide. "Are we going to get that kinky tonight?" I grinned.

"Well, maybe not that kinky. You lot have to sleep eventually. However, I'm not average either. I don't want to hurt you."

I smiled. "For your knowledge, it's red. And if you say red, everyone will stop. Okay?"

"Sounds good," he said as we took my shirt off.

I glanced at the guys, and they were ahead of us. Ian already had Jason's dick in his mouth. I kissed Chuck again and unbuttoned his shirt. He was already hard, and his dick brushed my leg. "Oh, my."

He laughed softly. "Still interested?"

"Absolutely." I stood and unzipped my jeans, dropping them to the floor and kicking them away. The red lace underwear was bright against my skin in the low light. I had bought them specifically for this trip.

Chuck moved to reposition himself on the L-shaped couch. When he held out his hand, I took it, and he turned me around to look at Ian and Jason. I realized then he had positioned us so they could watch us, too.

I sat on his lap, and he spread my legs with his. It didn't take much since his thighs were massive. I leaned against his bare chest, and he reached to cup a breast in one hand and my pussy with his other. Like the massage earlier, he worked slowly, feeling things out. When his fingers dipped into my underwear to tease me, I sucked in enough air to gasp.

"I need to work you open more. If you can take three of my fingers, you'll be able to take me just fine," he said, as one finger worked inside me, and his thumb toyed with my clit.

Jason watched as Ian continued lavishing attention on Jason's cock. In no time, one finger progressed to two, and I ground my pussy into his hand. My moans triggered something for the guys and Jason came in Ian's mouth. I watched as Ian licked him clean and Jason relaxed. I must have sounded desperate, because Ian came over to me and dropped in front of us. He was still hard, and I made hand motions and tiny begging sounds, wanting Ian's dick either in my hand or in my mouth, but he had other plans.

Chuck responded by moving his thumb from my clit to let Ian have it. Ian's tongue and Chuck's fingers were working me into a ball of pleasure that needed a release. Jason knew. He watched me, watched my face, until I gasped to take enough air to beg.

"Please . . ." was all I said.

Jason smiled. "Now, Ian."

Ian's fangs pierced my labia, and I came all over Chuck's fingers, soaking them, his shorts, splashing Ian, who lapped it up. Once that happened, Chuck moved quickly to insert his third and fourth fingers, working me to keep my orgasm going. I trembled with pleasure between Ian's licking and sucking, and Chuck's finger thrusts.

When Ian finally backed away, Chuck slowed as I leaned against him. I watched as Ian undid his slacks and tossed them and his boxers aside. Jason grabbed Ian's hips and pulled the man toward him. We watched as Jason removed a butt plug and then positioned himself so Ian could sit on him. As Ian's ass swallowed Jason's cock, he groaned in pleasure. I felt Chuck's dick twitch, and a small snicker of laughter slipped out.

"Wanna give it a go?" I asked.

"Sure," Chuck said as he helped me stand, and he pushed off his shorts until they pooled at his feet. I took off my panties and tossed the soaked garment onto the floor. Once that was taken care of, Chuck brought me back to his lap. His cock, along with several piercings, brushed against my ass and pussy. "I have protection."

"That's a good idea, in case something tears and I bleed. Though if that happens, I'll come anyway. So win-win there."

"Ah." He leaned down to pull a large, square foil packet out of a pocket. "You need pain, huh?"

"Yes. Is that alright?"

"I got you." He grinned. "Here, lean forward so I can slip this on." I crouched above him until he rolled on his condom. I assumed he'd go for it right then, but instead he slipped himself between my legs again and grabbed my thighs, pressing them closed around his cock. He moved me like I was nothing, letting all those piercings glide along my pussy and ass.

Our pace matched theirs. Ian and Jason were in no hurry, and both of them were watching us with as much attention as they were paying each other. Jason played with Ian's cock as he slid up and down on Jason's dick. I reached between my legs to do the same with Chuck's.

The nodes and nodules of the piercings were just as prominent, even though they were covered with a protective barrier. After feeling him up a few times, he pulled me back against his chest again, then looped his arms under my thighs, lifting me easily. His hand disappeared between my legs, and I felt him insert two fingers, but the third was a challenge. Apparently, my body had tightened back up after my long orgasm.

"We'll take it slow. Tell me if you need me to slow down, or stop," he said.

"Okay," I responded after taking a breath.

His fingers disappeared and my pussy clenched on air until he pressed the enormous head of his cock into me. He let me control how fast my body took on his cock. When I reached maybe half a dozen centimeters, I moaned so hard I nearly bit through my lip.

"You doing alright?" he asked.

"Yes, yes, fuck, yes."

Ian had stopped moving while Jason continued to play with him, watching me with Chuck. We often found others to play with while we were traveling together. This was the first time

Jason had seen me do anything with someone outside of our relationship or those we dated. They watched with rapt attention as I tried to take Chuck's cock.

"You can do it, sweetie. I want to see you take that whole thing until your abdomen bulges." I was about to tell Jason that it didn't work like that when more of Chuck slipped further into me, and I let out a whimper.

"Still with me, Mason?" Chuck asked.

I nodded. "Yes." He gently massaged as I continued to push myself onto him, or he was guiding me down. I wasn't sure which. The guys were suddenly full of movement. I heard a gasp and opened my eyes to see Ian come, then watched as Jason fucked him hard until he came. Watching them made me move my hips.

"Halfway there," Jason said as he cradled Ian against his chest, Jason's arms wrapped around Ian's torso. Their rapt attention was electrifying and slightly unnerving too, like some vampires could be when they were completely focused on you.

"Half? Holy shit," I moaned.

Chuck laughed. I moved my hips a little more, making him groan. I had just enough leverage to put my hands behind me, pushing off his chest, to reposition myself into a squat, thrusting onto him as his hands supported my hips. His soft groans turned into a long moan as he let me do what I wanted.

After several more thrusts, he pushed into me far enough I could feel the head of his dick pressed against my cervix. We paused for a moment so Chuck could catch his breath. I was mostly sitting on his lap with my feet planted on the sofa.

"Fuck, you're still tight. You sure you're okay?" Chuck asked as he panted.

"Sure, no. But I'm not stopping." I wasn't sure what he was going to do, but when his right hand lit on my clit, and his other hand went to a spot on my low back, just left of center, and pressed, then shifted around and pressed again. The orgasm I wasn't prepared for hit me like a high-speed transit. "Oh, fucking hell, shit!" I came. Then Chuck, who had patiently waited for me to adjust to him, grabbed my hips and used me like a fuck toy. I felt every one of his piercings rub spots I didn't know I had, and I swore I saw an impression of his cock outlined on my lower abdomen. Or my uterus trying to escape the onslaught of Chuck's much faster pace. When he finally came, I was raw and too sensitive to move. Chuck's dick, even half-hard, still filled me.

My eyes closed, and I wasn't aware of anything but the hum of my body until Jason kissed me on the lips. "You still with us, Mason?"

"Mmm hmm." I smiled.

"Is it okay if Chuck takes you to the bathroom to clean up? Ian's fading, and it's almost sunrise."

"It's okay." They laughed because my words were obviously slurred. Jason kissed me again, then he spoke quietly with Chuck. I was beyond words and not the least bit concerned with what they were saying.

The orc lifted me off him slowly, and I felt every centimeter leave my body. He moved with ease, carrying me to the bathroom, where he set me on the small bench in the shower. I leaned against the wall as he turned on the water. I cracked my eyes open and watched as he soaped himself up. He caught me looking and smiled, then asked a question.

"Jason said you could stay awake after daybreak. Are you a dhampir?"

I shook my head. "Something different, but we let people think I am. It's safer that way." I don't know why I told him that. For some reason, I trusted him, and I had only met him today.

We were quiet for a time while I watched him finish cleaning up. "Your turn." He took a washcloth and used the body wash nearby to create a decent lather. His large hands were an experience as he used a soft cloth to scrub me down from neck to feet. When he wiped between my legs, the washcloth came away with blood on it. "Uh, Mason?"

He showed me, and I carefully took the towel away from him. "Wash your hands with soap." Chuck did as instructed, and I finished cleaning myself.

Once we were drying off, I could feel him watching me. "It's okay, I'm not bleeding. See?" I showed him the dry towel, and he looked a little more relieved.

"I know vampires and shifters can heal pretty quickly." What was unspoken in that statement was that those were likely his preferred partners for just that reason.

"It was likely a small tear, quick to heal. I assure you I'm fine." He nodded as he tugged on his shirt. Jason must have brought Chuck's clothes to the bathroom and even spelled them clean. He was very considerate like that. Ian would have done the same if he had been awake.

Chuck noticed I didn't have any clothes and handed me a robe, then he pulled on his pants. Once I had the robe tied shut, I moved closer to Chuck. He smiled as he slipped on his loafers. "Are you okay?" I asked.

"Yeah." He smiled. "I had an awesome night with a lady friend and her partners. Who are fucking hot, by the way. I'm a little envious."

That made me grin as he stood and opened his arms. I put my arms around his waist and snuggled in. "We've been through a lot together. There's a lot of love between us."

"I'm happy there was enough left to share," Chuck said.

"Always." I lifted my head and smiled up at his chin, then stepped back to look him in the eyes. "They like to indulge me."

"Well, I hope you enjoyed tonight. I know I did."

"I did too."

We walked out of the bathroom and into the hall toward the doors to the suite. This one had a double set. The internal doors had to be shut before the external doors could open. It prevented daylight from coming into the room.

Chuck opened the interior door and stopped to look at me. "If your group ever comes this way again, let me know." He pressed a card into my hand. "I'd be happy to entertain you all for a weekend." He gave me a salacious look with the comment.

"We'll keep that in mind." I smiled and tucked the card away in my robe. He nodded.

"May I give you a kiss goodbye, Mason?" I silently agreed by nodding. Chuck leaned down and planted a gentle kiss on my lips, mindful of his tusks. "Sleep well and enjoy the rest of your stay."

"Thank you. Have a good day, Chuck." We gave each other a little wave as he left.

I waited until the lock cycled and I heard the other door open before I walked back to our bedroom. My guys were already passed out and curled up with each other. I dropped my robe and the towel around my hair, then climbed into bed with them, content to sleep the rest of the day and eager to see what the night would bring.

M. L. Eaden
Scales n Art

THE SAINT GEORGE CHRONICLES

Author's Note
Pride of The Lyndon Family

I wrote this short story for an author promotional event for Pride 2023. While I knew Greg's backstory, and some about his childhood, this opportunity gave me a chance to address a couple of *cough* plot *cough* holes. Mainly, how did Greg have Jennifer for a first grade teacher, but was also homeschooled for most of his primary education? Divorce isn't ever a fun situation to be in, and it's even worse when you've married into a family with a lot of power and money.

If you're wondering about another minor detail when Greg mentions his half-siblings, don't worry, it'll come up again in book four.

You'll also note that I wrote this in third-person omniscient. I'm used to writing in first-person subjective and thought it was a neat challenge for myself to see if I could write in a different voice.

Content Warnings: *off-page verbal abuse, discussion of divorce proceedings*

PRIDE OF THE LYNDON FAMILY

WASHINGTON STATE - 1976

Philip came into Gregor's room and locked the door behind him. Gregor had heard yelling and things being thrown. He looked up from his toys and saw that his dad looked scared.

"Son, I need you to pack a few things. We're going to stay with Grandpa Jack for a few days." Gregor's dad went to his closet and pulled down his suitcase.

"Grandpa Jack?" His words were precise, as much a three-year-old's soft palate would allow.

"Yes, baby. We're going to visit Grandpa Jack." Philip put Gregor's suitcase on the bed. "Here, pick a few toys and a book or two while I pack your clothes."

Gregor picked a small teddy bear and a dragon he liked to sleep with. The books he picked were about a big red dog, and another about fairies. Philip indicated he should put his toys and books in with his clothes. Once he did, Philip closed the suitcase.

"There. All set. Let's go, shall we?"

"Say bye-bye to mommy?"

"No baby, not this time." Gregor cried as Philip picked him up, carrying him the entire way to the garage and loaded them into his vehicle. The safety seat gave Gregor a view of his home as they drove away. He cried, unable to express his confusion. Eventually, the vibrations of the vehicle lulled him into a fitful sleep.

SAN FRANCISCO - 1979

The last time Gregor saw his mother, he was three. He missed her sometimes, but didn't remember her face. Grandpa Jack was nice but hard of hearing, and his dad worked a lot. There wasn't much to do around the house except read or play with toys. Sometimes Grandpa would turn on the flat screen and they would watch his picture shows.

For most of his young life, all Gregor knew was the house, the backyard, the wood shop, and Holden.

Holden came to clean Grandpa's house every Monday, Wednesday, and Friday. Gregor would follow him around asking questions while Holden did chores. Holden would answer with stories while he started the various machines that cleaned the floors, the walls, and laundry. They seemed inseparable, no matter how much his dad and grandpa tried to get Gregor to leave him alone. Holden didn't mind. He thought Gregor was a good kid who needed a little more structure than his father could provide, considering the circumstances.

"How much did you learn today, Gregor?" Holden asked as they sorted clean clothes and folded them.

"Lots. We learned numbers. The alphabet. I made a picture for you," Gregor said as he pulled a piece of yellow paper made of bamboo out of his pocket.

Holden unfolded the paper to reveal a large orange sun with a rainbow under it. The clouds were blue, outlined in white. In the middle of the paper, there was a stick figure that had "Holden" written above it. Another smaller stick figure said "Gregor," who was holding hands with a red stick figure with yellow wings named "Francis."

"Well, this is pretty. Who's Francis?" Holden asked.

"My dragon." Gregor sighed. "Dad won't let me take him to school, so I draw him a lot. See?" Gregor pulled out another picture that had more details. In this one, Francis had a belly that was yellow and red flames coming out of his mouth.

"Francis seems pretty scary."

"He protects me."

"From what?"

"Angry people."

Holden folded up the larger picture of Francis and gave it back to Gregor. "Then you should keep this picture with you, so you'll always have Francis around in case you run into any angry people." Gregor nodded and stuck the picture in his pocket. Before Holden put away the other drawing, he showed off a little.

"Have you ever seen magic, Gregor?"

"On the screen. In some of Grandpa's shows."

"Watch this." Holden folded the paper in half, closed his eyes, and said a few words Gregor didn't understand. When he opened the page, the stick figures danced, and the rainbow was flashing colors, making fireworks in the paper sky. Gregor was instantly enchanted.

Over the few years that Philip and Gregor lived with Jack, Holden became part of their family. He would stay for dinners, play with Gregor when his dad was busy, even walk him home from school. Gregor loved his time with Holden because it meant they could talk about dragons, magic, and school. His father was interested sometimes, but work distracted him a lot. Grandpa Jack always talked about trees and wood, which were important, but boring to a seven-year-old.

On a pretty summer day, Holden and Gregor were drawing on the sidewalk with chalk, making all kinds of animals. Gregor was busy working on some clouds when Holden asked about school.

"So, Gregor, are you looking forward to first grade?"

Gregor shrugged. "I guess."

"You guess? What about your friends from last year?"

He shrugged again. "You're my friend, Holden."

Holden frowned. "That's true. I am. But don't you want to make some friends your own age?"

"Why do I need to make friends if you're my friend?" Gregor asked. There was a long pause before Gregor looked up at Holden. They both stopped drawing.

"Come sit next to me, buddy," Holden said. Gregor stood, and Holden looked up at him. The kid was lanky and maybe too pale from being indoors too much. Holden patted the grass next to him. Gregor jumped over the drawing and landed next to Holden, spinning, then sitting on the exact spot he'd pointed out.

Gregor smiled at Holden, waiting. Holden hated himself a little because he was probably about to chase the smile from Gregor's face. "I've had a lot of fun, Gregor. And we'll still be friends, but I won't be around after the school year starts."

"Why not?" Gregor looked confused.

"I'm going back to school, too. But the school isn't here. It's pretty far away."

"How far?" Gregor's face was blank, but his brown eyes were alight, calculating, curious. Trying to understand what Holden meant.

"Far enough that I won't be able to work for your grandpa any more."

"Oh." There was a touch of disappointment there before it disappeared. "How many days before you leave?"

"A few more weeks."

"And you'll work for Grandpa Jack until then?"

"Yep."

"Okay."

"If you have questions, you can ask me." Holden offered, concerned that Gregor hadn't understood what he said.

"Okay." Gregor moved back to his original spot and picked up his chalk. They continued drawing. Gregor was quiet until Holden made the chalk picture move with a bit of magic, like he had many times before. All Gregor wanted to understand was that Holden wasn't leaving tomorrow. His chest hurt when he thought about Holden leaving at all, so he tried not to. It was easier that way.

On Holden's last day with the Lyndon's, he gave everyone a hug before he left. Everyone was a little sad about Holden leaving. Gregor most of all. After Holden left, Gregor went to his room and cried, but didn't quite understand why he was so sad.

The following Monday, his dad walked him to school like he usually did. "First day of first grade. How are you feeling about it?"

"Okay, I guess."

"You guess? This is an adventure! New friends to make, people to meet. You'll see."

Gregor frowned and shuffled along beside his dad. "Who's going to walk me home?"

"I will," Philip said.

Gregor looked up at him, frown turning to a worry. "You won't forget?" He knew his dad's work was important. He helped make things with computers.

"Not on purpose. I put a reminder on my desk." The frown didn't leave Gregor's face with Philip's reassurance. Philip reached out and touched Gregor's arm, turning Gregor to look at him. "I mean it. It was great having Holden around to help, but I'm your parent. I should be the one to make sure you get to and from school."

"It's not that far. I can go by myself."

"No. Someone should walk with you. I should walk with you. Get a little exercise and breathe the air instead of being in my office."

"Okay. If you say so." Greg shrugged.

Philip laughed softly. "I do say so." They resumed walking until they reached the school. The front lawn was full of parents and kids meeting their teachers before going inside. His dad pointed out an adult holding a sign that said "first grade."

"Morning." The woman said as they walked up. "I'm Miss MacTavish. And who might you be?" She didn't address his father, she addressed Gregor. He wasn't used to adults paying much attention to him.

"Gregor Lyndon, ma'am."

"Do you like to be called Gregor or Greg?" Miss MacTavish asked.

"Greg, ma'am." He had never been called Greg before, but he liked it the instant she had asked.

"How delightful to meet you, Greg." She put out her hand. Gregor took it and gave her the best handshake a seven-year-old could manage. "Do you know which pronouns you'd prefer to use?"

"Pronouns?" Greg repeated.

"Yes. I prefer she and her. Are yours him, her, them, or something else, perhaps?"

No one had ever asked him before. He hadn't even realized he had a choice until Miss MacTavish asked about his name. "Oh. I'm a him, ma'am."

"Good to know." Miss MacTavish turned to his dad. "And you are?" She asked.

"Philip Lyndon, his father. We spoke on the phone. Pleased to meet you, Miss MacTavish." Greg watched as the two shook hands, then acted a little weird. Sheesh. Adults.

A few weeks into the school year, Miss MacTavish introduced Greg to Mx. Hun, the school counselor. Greg wondered what he might have done to land him in the counselor's office.

"Have a seat, Greg," Mx. Hun offered. They were shorter than Miss MacTavish and had kind dark eyes, white hair on their head and chin. They wore a light linen buttoned shirt and slacks with shoes that looked like slippers. He'd never seen an adult look so casual besides his grandpa. Considering his grandpa was retired, it seemed acceptable.

Greg walked over to a comfortable chair that swiveled. He played with the knobs and adjusted the height until his feet dangled, then dropped it back down again. Mx. Hun didn't seem to mind any of it, just watched until he settled.

"Is there anything you'd like to talk about?" Mx. Hun asked.

Greg shook his head. If Mx. Hun wouldn't bring it up, he'd keep his mouth closed. Upon rotating the chair to face away from the desk, something caught Greg's gaze. An intricate depiction of an eastern dragon flying through a cloud-filled mountain landscape with other dragons hiding amongst them.

"Do you like the painting?" Mx. Hun asked.

Greg nodded. "They're different from Francis, but I like them."

"Who's Francis?"

"My dragon."

"What kind of dragon is Francis?"

"A European dragon."

"Like this?" Mx. Hun snapped their fingers, and a light pulsed from their index finger. As Greg watched, they drew a European dragon with spread wings, using only a stream of light.

It fascinated Greg. He reached out to touch the dragon. It shimmered, then burst into sparkles of light, making Greg giggle. Mx. Hun laughed with him.

"Want to try it?"

"How?" Greg was curious. Doctors had tested him for magic abilities. The one that mattered to his mother wouldn't activate until he was thirteen, so she said.

"Hold out your index finger." Greg did as Mx. Hun instructed. They touched their index finger to Greg's, immediately making it glow. Greg waved it in the air, and a stream of colorful light followed.

They played with the light streams until a small timer went off on Mx. Hun's desk. "That's all the time we have for today. Would you like to come back tomorrow, Greg?"

Greg nodded, looking forward to next time with Mx. Hun. He reminded Greg of Holden, who he missed terribly. His index finger stopped glowing when he passed through Mx. Hun's door. Miss MacTavish was there waiting for him.

"Can you find your way back to class, Greg?" Miss MacTavish asked.

Greg nodded to her and waved to Mx. Hun as he left. "See you tomorrow, Mx. Hun."

"See you tomorrow, Greg."

Once the boy was out of hearing range, Miss MacTavish turned to Mx. Hun. "Any thoughts on how to help him?"

"He's closed off. Very protective, but curious. I think if he knows it's safe to be himself, he'll be less wary." Mx. Hun paused, thinking. "How supportive is his father?"

"Very." Miss MacTavish said. "He ended his marriage to protect him. There's a pretty heavy ongoing custody case. His father has kept the details from Greg. From what he's shared with me, he took Greg after a pretty intense argument about Greg holding hands with a boy at his daycare. His mother was fairly upset, while Philip thought it was an innocent thing and saw nothing wrong with it since they were only three-years-old. The argument escalated from there."

"Philip, hmm." Mx. Hun gave Miss MacTavish a knowing look.

"Mr. Lyndon cares about his son's well being. Given the type of environment Greg was in, it's a valid concern. I think he did the right thing."

Mx. Hun nodded. "A school with multiple species, genders, and identities will continue to challenge him. However, I think his curiosity will see him through and allow him to adapt. He's a smart kid with a good heart and might even become a natural leader among his peers."

"That's encouraging. Was that from reading his aura?" Miss MacTavish asked.

"No." Mx. Hun smiled. "It was from his index finger." They wiggled their index finger at Miss MacTavish. They laughed and spoke a few more minutes before Miss MacTavish returned to her classroom.

In Greg's kindergarten year, most kids looked like kids. They were all too young to shift or have abilities. That changed in first grade. While everyone in his class had human traits, most of them were not human. While it caught him off-guard some-times, he learned not to react.

Others could shift into various animals or had traits that were visible because one parent was mostly human and the other was a shifter. What surprised him the most were those that should be opposed to one another based on traits, but behaved and even got along with each other. Feline and Canine shifters played games and often worked together to solve problems, using the advantages they had.

The kid that interested him the most was Jake Collins. He was twice Greg's size and napped all the time. Miss MacTavish didn't yell at him for being tired, or admonish him when he fell asleep during lessons. Jake ran out of energy all the time, though when he was awake, his dark brown eyes took in everything. Greg thought that could be because he was a bear shifter.

One day during another math lesson, Jake's face shifted when he nodded off. Greg tried not to stare. He couldn't help his fascination with jake's adorable brown bear's face. A couple of kids snickered as Jake softly snored, but Greg kept glancing at him while he slept, wondering if Jake would shift back when he woke up.

He kept sneaking glances throughout the Math lesson until Greg glanced again and realizing Jake had caught him. Their eyes met and Greg quickly looked away as a panicked, nervous energy shot through him. It wasn't a good idea to panic in a room full of kids with budding abilities. The longer Jake stared at him, which he knew because Greg kept sneaking glances, the more anxious Greg became. He hadn't meant to offend Jake. He was only curious.

Greg saw other students sniffing the air, probably trying to find the source of anxiety. He knew if he got up and tried to leave, it could turn the whole classroom into a large and possibly not friendly game of tag. He'd seen it before on the playground. What might have started friendly changed the moment any kid's scent shifted. Once it turned into something all the predators recognized as fear or prey, things turned a little more dangerous for those that lacked abilities. The teachers would wade in to break it up. Kids would come out with scratches and bruises, but nothlng worse.

Recognizing his predicament, Greg put down his stylus and focused on the math problem. He recited the numbers under his breath, breathing in slowly, holding it for a count of four, then letting it out like Mx. Hun had taught him. He kept repeating the process until he felt calm again. The tension in the room eased and when he glanced at Jake, Greg noticed he'd returned to napping.

Crisis averted, Greg focused on the example on the interactive board at the front of the class Miss MacTavish had just finished.

"Can anyone solve this problem?" She asked.

Greg tapped the desk and minimized his assigned homework to look more closely at the problem on the board. A few kids raised their hands and so did he. Miss MacTavish saw him.

"Greg, you can try to solve the problem. Remember to show your work." It was a fairly simple subtraction. One hundred fifty-two from fifty. He completed the problem, looking up to make sure his work appeared on the interactive board in front of the class. Miss MacTavish drew a smiley face next to the problem. "Excellent work, Greg. Let's try another one." She erased his work and wrote another problem on the board. "Tracy, how about you take this one?"

The math lesson ended, and Greg pulled his homework up to work on it until lunchtime. He heard Jake move and tried not to look. A note popped up on his desk from Jake. "Could you help me with math?" Greg looked up and saw the sleepy face practically pleading with him. He smiled, stood, then walked the few steps to Jake's desk. He was struggling with today's lesson.

"What part do you need help with?" Greg asked.

"I can't remember whether a zero becomes a 9 or a 10 here," replied Jake.

"An easy way to remember is if the zero is on the end, it's a ten."

"Why is that?"

Greg shrugged. "Because you can't subtract a number from zero. And it borrows ten from the number on the left."

"Huh?"

"Yeah, I'm not sure why either." The boys laughed. "Maybe Miss MacTavish can help?" Jake nodded, and they pressed the button on his desk to alert their teacher.

She showed up at Jake's desk after helping another student. "What can I help with?"

Jake still didn't understand why the numbers worked the way they did, but eventually he worked through each problem as their teacher helped. Once his homework was done, Greg returned to his desk to finish his homework. When the bell rang for lunch, his classmates were leaving while Greg was still working on his last few problems until Jake stood next to him.

"Aren't you hungry?" Jake asked.

"Yes, but I want to finish my homework first," said Greg.

"There's always homework. No wonder you're so tiny. Come on. Let's get lunch. Finish that later."

Greg glanced at Miss MacTavish. She nodded to him with a smile. It was hard for him to not finish his assignments. There were plenty of times Miss MacTavish pushed him out the door for lunch or recess, telling him to finish it later.

Jake wrapped a warm hand around Greg's arm. "It's pizza day. We can't miss pizza day."

Greg laughed as he stood. "The witches in the cafeteria make sure there's enough food for everyone. They won't run out."

"Says you. It happened once. Bobby Travis said they ran out of pizza and only had Brussels sprouts with cheese for the rest of lunch. They're okay, but I like pizza more. Come on." Jake gently pulled on his arm.

"Okay, okay. I'm coming." The two talked about food all the way to the cafeteria.

After that day, Jake and Greg were fast friends. Later, when their parents picked them up, discovering they both lived in the same neighborhood, Philip invited Jake and his parents for dinner a few nights later, much to Greg's surprise.

"They're here!" Greg called out. Both the older Lyndon men were busy prepping things in the kitchen. Greg watched as Jake and his parents, Linus and Stephen Collins, walked up to the door. Greg had the door open before anyone could knock.

"HI," he said as he looked at the three of them standing on the porch. Jake was a miniature of Stephen, who was tall, blond, and bulky. Linus was shorter with brown hair and glasses.

Jake and Greg were already the tallest in their class, though Jake weighed more than him by at least ten kilos. Bear shifters were always large, so Jake said. And they liked to eat. Mostly fish, but they would eat whatever Greg's family cooked, so Jake said.

Philip came up behind Greg and put a hand on his shoulder. "You want to let our guests in?"

"Right, sorry, come in." Greg opened the door wider so everyone could come in. Jake was inside first, followed by his dads. Philip shook their hands in welcome, then introduced them all to Grandpa Jack, who had brought the adults beers and root beers for Jake and Greg.

"Greg, how about you show Jake your room while we finish up dinner?" Philip suggested.

"Sure." Greg looked at Jake. "It's this way," he said with a nod of his head.

Jake followed Greg down a short hallway to his room. They sat on Greg's bed next to each other.

"Have any comics?" Jake asked.

"Sure." Greg pulled out a portable desk and turned it on. He tapped an icon and several other icons showed up, displaying which comics were available. "It doesn't hold very much, and they are in black and white. I have to plug it into the house line to get more. My dad says they are coming out with color desks and those will have more memory."

"That's cool. Have you ever seen real comics?"

Greg shook his head. Those weren't cheap. His father didn't have the extra money. He counted himself lucky to have a black and white portable desk that he could read stuff and practice math homework, and that was only because of his dad's job.

"My daddy collects them. He has these special boxes he keeps them in. Won't let me touch them. It sucks," Jake said.

"Which dad is that?"

"Linus. The one with hair on his face." Jake scratched his chin as if he was imitating his dad. "My other dad likes to collect tools."

"Cool. My dad and grandpa have a wood shop. They have lots of tools in there."

"A wood shop?" Jake's eyebrows were nearly lost in his blond bangs. "Is your dad an ent?"

Greg laughed. "Do we look like ents?"

"Okay, fine. You don't really smell like one either." They both read another comic strip before Jake's curiosity got the best of him. "But how do you have a wood shop if you're not an ent?"

"Grandpa was an arborist." Jake looked at him funny. "That's a person who helps trees." Jake gave a slight nod, and Greg continued. "When the ents and the trees around them have downed limbs, they would give them to Grandpa sometimes,"

Greg said with a shrug. "Then he makes things with the wood and sells them. He's retired now. He takes my dad sometimes to visit an ent group close by on the weekends. They still give us wood pieces, even though Grandpa doesn't practice any longer."

"That's cool. I've never heard of ents trusting humans," said Jake. "Where my grandparents live, ents like to move and mess up the trails. Humans can't tell and get lost in the woods. Local shifters go out to rescue them. Sometimes the ents will leave a hiker alone, but only if they leave a present."

"Geez, I wouldn't want to hike in those woods."

"Don't worry. You'll be with me. They don't bother bears. Ents can't mess with our trails like they can human ones."

Greg wondered what that meant exactly, but just then, Philip knocked on his door and opened it. "Dinner time, guys." They jumped up, leaving the desk on Greg's bed to follow his dad into the kitchen where everyone crowded in, happily chatting.

Dinner was mostly a conversation between the grownups. Jake ate everything Linus put on his plate and Greg watched with fascination as loads of veggies disappeared while he had barely started his.

"We're on the local Pride committee this year. Are you planning to go? It's in June." Stephen asked as he made a pile of spaghetti on his plate, then poured a ladle of sauce over the top. He added cheese while Linus continued.

"We're also on the PTA and talked the school board into letting us use the entire school building for the day," Linus said.

"The teachers even volunteered to run some of the game booths. We're having a talent show, and a cake and pie walk," said Stephen.

"And a big raffle with donations from folks in the neighborhood," Linus added.

Greg's adults were quiet as they ate and listened. He noticed a glance between the two and a slight nod.

"We'd be happy to donate something from our wood shop," Greg's dad offered.

All eating stopped for a moment as Linus and Stephen looked at Philip. "You have actual carved wood pieces?" Linus asked.

"They're all ethically sourced. We can provide a certificate. That way, anyone that ends up with the piece can legally have it," Grandpa Jack said.

Jake's parents exchanged a look of their own before Linus agreed. "That would definitely be a crowd pleaser. It wouldn't contain magic, would it?"

Grandpa Jack shook his head. "We only use the wood given to us, and only if it's detached from the body of the group. There might be some residual essence of spirit, but nothing anyone could draw from. Though for the right witch or mage, it could be a decent focus if they had some kind of elemental magic."

"What pieces do you think might do well for the raffle?" Philip asked.

"A set of bowls? Or maybe serving spoons. Things people can use and pass down to other family members," Grandpa Jack said.

"Any of that would be perfect," Linus said.

"After we finish up dinner, we can go to the shop and pick something out," Grandpa said with a smile. Greg smiled too because everyone seemed happy about helping. It was something he expected from his dad and grandpa and wanted to do the same when he grew up.

Jake broke up the conversation by slurping a bunch of noodles from his plate into his mouth and followed that up with loud smacking noises. His parents looked horrified.

"Young bear, we are not in the woods. Use your utensils," Stephen admonished. Jake frowned for a moment until he stuck his fork into his noodles, then swirled it until it was overflowing. Greg noticed and followed suit. They made a quiet contest of how many noodles they could keep on their forks as they shoveled them into their mouths.

His dad didn't say a word, just winked at him as he and Jake continued their contest of wills, which Greg lost. His stomach was only so big and was no match for a bear's. After Jake and his parents left, Greg went to clean up and get ready for bed. His dad knocked just as he was putting on his pajamas.

"Ready for bed?" Philip asked.

"Yep!"

"Want me to read tonight?" Greg nodded and climbed into bed. "Any requests?"

"Do we have anything about bears?"

Philip glanced at the tablet and frowned. "Nothing we have downloaded. And I think Grandpa might have a book or two, but those should probably wait until you're older."

Greg frowned. "I guess we could read the Hardy boys again."

Philip took a small case from a shelf and slipped out the first book in the series. The books were a present for his sixth birthday from his grandpa, made from bamboo pulp. It was very rare to have books made with wood pulp. Occasionally, Grandpa used some shavings from his workshop to make paper. He would sell it to a clairvoyant that used it to write up her visions. Dad thought Grandpa was sweet on her, but Grandpa never said one way or the other.

His dad opened the first book in the series and began, "Chapter one, the glowing beast. 'Oh, oh, look who's here, said Frank Hardy.'"

Greg and Jake finished their first-grade year, and planned what they would do with their summer months. Their parental types even shared a few more meals together, and let the kids have sleepovers. They heard all about the planning for the Pride festival as the day grew closer.

The day of the Pride Festival, Greg was excited. Jake talked about it like it was one of the best days of the year. The Lyndon family walked together down the street to the school, while Greg tried to contain his nervous excitement. Once inside the school doors, he couldn't believe his eyes. The school was decorated in primary colors, with rainbows and peace symbols everywhere.

A sign at the entrance talked about the colors and why the LGBT community had adopted the rainbow a year before. The colors meant different things. Red for life. Orange for healing. Yellow for sunlight. Green for nature. Blue for serenity. Violet for spirit.

An interactive history lesson decorated the main entry hall to the school. There were pictures of important people, like Harvey Milk and others through history, that were part of the LGBT community. Each person's display had a story about their work helping communities gain greater acceptance of all species, cultures, and identities.

There was also a memorial to several local folks that were suffering from a new illness. It was called AIDS. All the medicine, science, and magic fields had come together to make a cure for the virus, but it was proving tricky. While there wasn't a cure yet, they made great strides in experimental medicines that helped control symptoms and kept the virus in check.

Greg stayed in the hall for a long time, reading information displays even as others went to play games. His grandpa stayed with him as he read while his dad went to find Jake's parents.

"What's on your mind, kiddo?" Grandpa Jack asked.

Greg looked at his grandpa with a frown. "The people on these displays were good people. Trying to help others. Why would people hate them?" Jake had mentioned that people gave his parents a hard time. It made little sense to Greg. They were good people and loved their son.

"Well, some people fear what they don't understand. They think that if they express their hate, and harm those that try to help, then others will stop helping or hide. What they don't realize, Greg; anything born of hate doesn't survive. It's a poor foundation for growth. Eventually, it eats itself alive."

His grandpa's words made Greg sad and anxious. "What can I do, grandpa?"

Greg heard his grandpa sigh softly. "You use your abilities for good, no matter what. Even if it means not using them at all."

Greg understood. "I swear, Grandpa." His grandpa patted his shoulder and turned Greg around, his brown eyes catching Greg's gaze as he knelt down.

"That's all I can ask. Protect those that can't protect themselves. Love those that can't manage for themselves and always try to help." Greg nodded, easily agreeing with all his eight-year-old heart. "Now, let's go find your dad and see if we can win ourselves a cake."

Across the gym and down another hall, Philip hadn't found Jake's parents, but he had found a face he remembered. "Miss MacTavish!" Philip called out as he saw her working the horseshoe tossing booth.

"Mr. Lyndon! Hello. Where's Greg?"

"He's with my father reading the historical displays in the main hall."

She smiled. "Greg has a curious mind. Reads a lot for his age. It was hard to find things to keep him interested."

"That's my Greg." Philip smiled back at Miss MacTavish.

"I was wondering, Mr. Lyndon." She paused for a moment, taking a quick breath and looking around, clearly a little nervous. "Would you be interested in going on a date with me?" There was another pause as Philip processed the question, surprised by it. "I wanted to ask sooner, but I thought it was inappropriate while Greg was in my class. I thought it might make it easier to say yes if I waited."

She smiled at him and saw that he had a phone. She pointed at it, and Philip handed it to her. He watched as she typed in her number. "Don't decide now. Think about it. Call me when you're ready."

Philip read her name and phone number, then saved it. Jennifer MacTavish. Several kids got into line for the horseshoe toss, and Jennifer turned to help them. Philip was smiling as Greg and Jack walked up.

"Hi Dad! Hi Miss MacTavish!" Greg said.

Jennifer turned to see who called her name while she was helping another player with the horseshoe game. "Hi Greg. Having a good summer?"

"Yes, ma'am."

"That's good to hear. Wanna play?" Greg nodded and got in line. Jennifer winked at Philip. His father caught the exchange.

"What was that about?"

Philip showed Jack his phone, and Jack chuckled with a smile. "Definitely like her better than the last one."

"You haven't really met her yet. How could you know?" Philip asked his father.

Jack smiled. "Anyone that understands your son will understand you. He's questioning things, Philip. If your lady friend sticks around, he might be a halfway decent person despite your ex wife's best efforts."

"I hope so. This is the last summer I'll have him. After they file the court order, I'll only see him every other weekend and during the summer until he's eighteen." While the thought of making Greg spend time with his ex wife bothered him, the best he could do was make sure Greg was prepared for it.

Greg ran up to his dad and grandpa. "Look, look! I won a bear!" He held up the small, handmade stuffed toy. "It's so cute! It looks like Jake when he's sleeping in class." The older Lyndons laughed.

"Should we go find Jake and see if he thinks so?" Philip asked.

Greg realized what he said and frowned. "Maybe I could just show him the bear?"

Philip and Jack shared a glance. "I don't think he's going to mind as much as you think he might. You're friends, yeah?" Philip asked.

"Yeah." Greg relaxed.

"Come on kiddo, let's go find your buddy," said Grandpa Jack. He put his arm around Greg's shoulders as they went to find Jake, Linus, and Stephen. The trio spent the evening with friends and came home with a chocolate cake, a stuffed bear, and one phone number from a very smitten teacher. All in all, it was a great first Pride festival for the Lyndon family.

A Saint George Chronicles Short Story

Fashion Statement

M.L. Eaden

Author's Note
Fashion Statement

Fashion Statement was something I did at the request of Tapas readers. I offered a hold-over short story while they were waiting for volume three. It gave me a chance to talk about an upcoming relationship that is heavily featured in *The Dragon's Egg*, and add some more about mages. When a guy studies dragons for most of his formative years, it's not like it leaves a lot of room for figuring out how other species and humans with abilities work beyond the obvious. At least that's my excuse, and I'm sticking to it.

FASHION STATEMENT

GREGOR

"I don't understand why we split up to do this. Couldn't we all have clothes made at the same place?" Jordan was dressed in tight jeans and a silk shirt that looked like it was woven around him instead of sewn together. For all I knew, it might have. Fae were interesting like that. You never knew exactly what they were capable of until they showed you, and Jordan rarely showed anyone. Though I had a feeling Xavior and I knew more than most.

"Unless you want to wear a floor length tunic, no. Xavior is being dressed by Jael. They practically begged, so I let them." That was interesting. Jordan had been very protective of Xavior, so much so that he'd taken to his den or went flying to have a break. The only time Jordan had left Xavior's side was if they were traveling, Jordan had to work, or Dr. Alexander was with Xavior. Which was exactly where she was at the moment. While Jordan was protective, he also used it as an excuse to visit Dr. Alexander. Apparently, they had started seeing each other. Considering Catherine was married, it was a slight surprise to me. The Alexander family had officially recognized Jordan as her consort only a few weeks ago.

Xavior tried to explain it to me. The basic gist was that mage families were half royalty and half commune. Because mages were long-lived, they tended toward multiple partners. Children were cared for communally, and the extramarital partners could assist in the child-rearing or leave it up to the mage family.

"We could have all worn tunics, or dresses, or whatever Jael comes up with." It was a quip, mostly. I hadn't ever worn a dress, but life had been interesting as of late, so wearing a dress would have been the least of my worries. The new clothes were for a movie premiere we were all attending in Los Angeles. My first as a stunt person.

"Fuck that. The trollop can fawn over Xavior and get their fill while they still can." Jordan pushed open the door to the shop he'd directed us to. I entered behind him, still wondering if I'd met Jael, and why Jordan had called them a trollop. Another fae greeted us. It was clear they knew each other, or there was mutual respect, because Jordan bowed to the fae. I followed Jordan's lead and did the same. She appeared to be a tailor, but I could only assume that until Jordan spoke to me in English.

The two fae carried on a conversation until it came to its natural conclusion. Jordan bowed again, and so did I.

"So, what happens next?" I whispered.

"We strip."

He placed a hand on my back and led me forward to a row of changing rooms. He pulled the curtain back to reveal a changing robe on one hook, a bench, and two empty hooks.

"You don't have to wear the robe if you're comfortable in your underwear. However, should you want your inseam to be accurate, I suggest you lose the boxer briefs." He gave me a light shove into the small room and pulled the curtain shut. I heard him move to the one next to me. A sigh escaped me as I undid my tie and worked on undressing. I took down the robe and pulled it on.

"This feels like a robe Xavior got me when we first started dating," I said as I walked out with the robe and my underwear on. No way did I want to be nude again in front of Jordan. His eyes took in everything, and it was hard to read exactly what he might be thinking unless he told you or his skin did. And I wasn't fluent enough in fae emotions to read his skin, though to look at him now, I would guess he was amused.

"Because it probably is a similar material. Xavior had your suit made here as well." The suit Jordan referred to was from Xavior's birthday party two years ago. I'd tried it on recently and the coat and shirt were snug in the shoulders and arms. The new job was demanding, and routines I had while I was a public safety officer seemed simplistic compared to the things I did now.

Jordan had a glass of something in his hand. His robe framed him nicely, and I tried not to think about Jordan and Xavior's past together. I wasn't jealous, exactly. Envious and curious were more accurate.

The tailor returned and pointed to a pedestal where Jordan stepped up and dropped his robe. Of course, he wasn't wearing underwear. I covered my face with my hand. Jordan chuckled at me. I had a three-sixty view thanks to the mirrors.

"Humans. Such prudes. Your virtue is safe with me, Gregor. Besides, we'd have to ask Xavior and the cohort of Alexander mages before we could do anything. Then they would have to agree on where and when."

I dropped my hand. "You're kidding."

"I am not. Being a consort is a very serious thing with mages."

"So you and Doc Alexander are that serious, huh?"

Jordan shrugged, but he had a smile on his face and his skin changed slightly from its normal pale-rose to a darker rose color. Not only was he serious, but by his skin tone, he had feelings for her as well. The tailor went about her work, drawing symbols in the air while moving Jordan around to take measurements. She conjured up several swathes of fabric before Jordan picked one.

Part of me didn't want to ask, but my curiosity got the better of me. "What about Xavior?"

"What about him?" Jordan's tone was curious, almost as if he didn't understand the question.

"Do you still have feelings for him?"

"Of course. Why would you wonder about that?"

"Well, your relationship with . . ."

"So narrow-minded," he said as he cut me off. "Regardless of your beliefs, there are many of us who can love and be with more than one individual at a time. Catherine is a magnificent person, as well as being a talented physician, mage, and mother. Why wouldn't someone want to desire and love her?"

"She's lovely, and I'm happy for you both, but I have to admit I'm confused."

"Confused about what?" He picked up his robe from the hook at the side of the mirror and slid it back on.

The tailor gestured for me to take Jordan's place. I did so and removed my robe, which she hung up. Then she proceeded to poke and prod at me. "What does that mean exactly, to be her consort? Ouch." Clearly, I needed to pay attention, or I could lose something important.

"Oh, that. Well, besides being an official status, it means we can fuck whenever we'd like. And her husband and his consort can watch or even participate if we so choose."

I had to be several shades of red because Jordan grinned at me, then picked up another flute glass of whatever he was drinking and took a sip.

"Should I explain emotional and sexual gratification to you as well, Gregor?"

"No, no, I get the picture."

"Do you? I could describe the last time we were all together, if you'd like."

He liked to push at what he thought were my shortcomings, such as my being monogamous. One dragon was enough for me, thank you. As I've come to know Jordan, I realize it was his way of teasing. "Jordan, I'm fine. No description necessary."

He let it go with a shrug, and I sighed until the tailor poked me in the thigh. She gestured for me to stand straight. I thought I was until she slapped my back and made me push out my chest.

"I do have to say, Gregor, your tone and definition are lovely. It was lovely before, but now it gives one imaginative ideas."

"Does Xavior talk about us with you?" Friends talk. Xavior likes to tell stories. How much did Jordan know already?

He shook his head. "No, and I would never ask him to. Unless that's something you'd like us to do. Some kind of kink, perhaps?"

Instead of dismissing him, I turned the idea over in my head. "It's a thought. I'll talk with Xavior about it." I wondered what Xavior might tell him, and what scene we could create, if Xavior was interested. Jordan clearly was, or he wouldn't have asked.

While I was monogamous, I knew Xavior wasn't by nature. We discovered that crafting scenes where others could be involved, but not physically there or intimate with us, helped.

"My, my, my, muscles and surprises. The two of you make more sense to me as time goes along."

"How so?" The question came out odd, as the tailor measured a somewhat sensitive place. She even pulled my boxer briefs up slightly to make sure it was accurate.

"You're considerate of each other. Even when one of you could decide on your own, you often consult each other to be sure. Plus, you both have a certain taste for rougher play."

The tailor handed me my robe, and I pulled it on.

"Oh, don't give me the 'how do you know' look, Gregor. The two of you mark each other enough to broadcast it to anyone paying attention."

I took a deep breath and sighed. "Maybe." While I tried to play it off, I had a smirk on my face. I liked it when Xavior wore my efforts of our mutual gratification. The only time Xavior made us cover any of it up was when we were with his family. Which, I admit, confused me slightly. I got the impression that they wouldn't care. Maybe he didn't want them to know how frequently we did things like that, but then again, I wasn't sure why Xavior cared. So I took a chance and asked a blunt question. "Jordan, why does Xavior cover it up if everyone knows and doesn't care?"

"Ah. That's an old habit he's probably not aware he still has. He used to hide Bianca's bites like that. Faith was particularly harsh on him when she found them."

Fuck. We were in therapy. It was important for both of us, but if I reminded him of Bianca? That wasn't good.

"If you were fae, your skin would be a nice, dark shade of blue right now." Jordan came closer. "It's not your fault. His relationship with that woman was his choice. What you are to each other is much different."

My gaze met his. "I know." I shrugged my shoulders and tried to let go of the tension I felt talking about Xavior's dead ex-fiancée.

"He's told me as much. But still. . ."

Jordan nodded. "Xavior is more fragile than he lets on. His skin is thick, but his heart is glass. You're the first of his lovers to see it, besides me. And I fear that sometimes, I wasn't all that careful with him either."

"If that were the case, he wouldn't keep you as close as he does. You're his best friend, and those aren't easy to come by, no matter who you are."

We went to the changing rooms to get dressed. When we walked out, the tailor stood waiting for us. She held a device in her hand, and Jordan thumbed it. They exchanged a few more words and bowed to each other. I bowed as well. Jordan turned and wrapped his arm around my shoulders and escorted me out.

"Maybe we need to work on finding a best friend for you. Someone that you respect, but also feel comfortable with." He patted my back and then let go of me as we walked back to his vehicle.

"Is there a spell for that?" With the new job and Xavior's pregnancy, I didn't have a lot of time for myself. Plus, I suspected I'd have even less after the whelp was born.

"Possibly," Jordan said with a light air of teasing to it.

"Really?"

"No, Gregor." He smiled. "Spells can't create genuine friendships or relationships. You do that on your own." I groaned, and Jordan laughed. "Oh, don't be so discouraged. You have a whole family of dragons, me, and even mages that can help." Jordan shrugged. "You can't build your life around Xavior. You need to build it with him and be your own person."

"Have you been talking to my therapist?" She had said something similar not that long ago.

"No, dear Gregor. I'm only this smart because I've been around long enough to make many, many mistakes."

I reached out and touched Jordan's arm to stop him. He turned to look at me. I'd thought about this for a while now, and if anyone could help Xavior, it would be Jordan.

"I need a favor."

One of Jordan's eyebrows rose nearly to his hairline. "I know you're not that careless, so it must be serious. Why would you ask a favor of a fae?"

"Not just any fae, Jordan. You. I'm asking you for it because at some point, I'm not going to be here and Xavior will need help." I almost couldn't say it and looked away, then brought my gaze back to Jordan. "Help to keep going after me."

"After you die," Jordan clarified, and I nodded. Jordan looked away, then pinned me with his gaze. "It's his choice, Gregor. I can't force him to continue if he gives up."

"There's a protocol. It tricks the pheromones for a while and gives a dragon a better chance of survival after their mate passes on."

"Why would you want me to do this?"

"It's for him and our whelp." I searched Jordan's eyes for any hint that he was about to reject my offer. "At best, I have another sixty years with him. At some point, my body won't function. When I reach that point, I want him to have options."

"So you're bargaining access to him for his continued survival after you've left the mortal coil?" Jordan's skin turned blue and grew darker by the moment.

"No, I know the payment for this needs to come from me, and that Xavior can make his own choices in that regard. What I'm saying is that the opportunity will exist, and the protocol works better if the person taking it has a strong relationship with the dragon." Jordan stared at me for a long time before he spoke again.

"Very well, then. What do you offer in exchange for this favor?" His color began to return to its neutral state. I breathed a sigh of relief.

"I'll make you my mom's famous shortbread cookies, with my own hands, every time you visit, until you ask me not to."

Jordan grinned. "I must say, Gregor, that was very well done. You picked the one thing in all the world I might have desired from you."

"Besides my friendship?"

"I have that already, Gregor, and we both know it." He patted me on the shoulder.

"Come, let's drink to our agreement. I'll take the protocol as a favor to you, but I cannot promise that it will help Xavior."

"I understand. My only goal here is to give him the option. I fear that without it, he won't even consider other possibilities."

Jordan nodded. "Very well. And as your friend, you'll let me help you find another. You're too focused on Xavior."

There was a strong desire to point out that it was the pot meeting the kettle on that one, but I let it go. "I suppose?" I had no idea what Jordan had planned, but knowing him, it would be elaborate and most certainly something he could tease me about.

"Excellent." Jordan's grin grew wider, if that was possible. "Then let's drink, and I'll ask questions." I nodded to that as Jordan walked us to the nearest bar.

It was nice to know that I'd already made one friend. After this, the others were all bonuses.

XAVIOR
&
GREGOR

Author's Note
The End

While you may recognize some characters in this short story, it shouldn't necessarily be considered canon. It was something that came to mind as I was writing the second volume of The Saint George Chronicles. I wasn't sure if I'd ever use it or publish it. However, after writing *Fashion Statement,* I thought it would be an interesting bookend to Greg's requested favor.

To this day, this story always gives me a bittersweet feeling reading it, if it doesn't outright make me cry.

Content Warnings: *declining health of a partner, death, grief, and old age.*

THE END

GREGOR

My cane clicked along as we walked. The soft rhythm of it lulled me into a kind of fugue state, one with a memory of a groaning dragon in his den with a grandfather clock ticking away in the corner. The memory brought a smile to my face.

"What were you thinking about just then?"

I turned to Xavior. "Your den right before the twins were born."

"I think you remember more of it than I do. I mostly remember feeling like I'd eaten too much while being split open at the same time. Their egg was huge."

"That was surprising, given Katie and Elena's hatchlings. Though Elena's smaller than you, being a different dragon species." I chuckled. "Didn't Faith say something about Trevor's eggs always being larger, too?"

"I don't want to remember anything about Trevor's eggs," Xavior grumbled.

I laughed, and it turned into a wheeze before long. Xavior used his hand to smooth circles onto my back. I eventually waved him off. "I'm fine, I'm fine."

"We should have that cough checked again. It doesn't sound very good."

"I'm old, Xavior. That's what anyone would say. Besides, the fresh air helps. At least, that's what the last doctor told us."

We kept walking along the garden path. Much of it Xavior and his staff had planted over the years. When my overall health took a slide, we took up residence in a cottage on the corner of Xavior's larger estate. Sasha moved into our old brownstone after grad school. Everett took after Xavior and started wandering around a bit. Phil started a band, then toured with them, and hadn't stopped to breathe, let alone visit in almost ten years.

Katie, my sister, and Elena, her wife, moved to Arizona to be near more of Elena's family. We talk via holo sometimes, but Katie tires easily. She's three years younger than me, and being long-lived is not a family trait.

I wanted to exert myself some, so I'd get a good night's sleep since we'd have family from all over the planet here by tomorrow for my eighty-fifth birthday. We had moved back to the main estate for the time being to make it easier for everyone. For that reason alone, I was determined to continue with my plodding pace.

Xavior laced his fingers through mine. My anchor for each step we took together. I knew the day was drawing closer when he'd have to walk forward without me. We rounded a bend, and I noticed a hover cart with Edward in the driver's seat. "Xavior."

"It's a quarter kilometer further than yesterday. Besides, if you hadn't made it, I would have carried you."

I rolled my eyes. "You're horrible."

"I love you too, asshole." He smiled at me. "There's water and a protein snack on the cart. Kindly eat and drink as much as you can on our way back to the house."

"Ugh, you're worse than Mom was."

"Yeah, probably so." Xavior sighed. "She's not here to take care of you, and I am, plus I have her cookies back at the house."

"Really?" All forward motion stopped. He hadn't made those in a while. Until recently, I'd been the one to make them.

Xavior liked both my parents, but Jennifer especially. It had been twenty years since they passed, and Sasha had taken over making the family favorite unless Jordan came to visit. Then I made them or helped Xavior make them. That he made them himself was a surprise. Not that he couldn't, but baking wasn't one of his favorite things.

"Yup. Unless you stand here all day and Sasha and Everett find them first. They should be at the house soon." He blinked to check a display and their flight paths provided by retinal nanites. I'd seen the behavior enough to recognize it.

"Okay then old man, we'd better get a move on." He laughed and followed me when he realized I'd walked ahead of him. Xavior was four hundred-twenty-six, but barely looked forty-five, if a day. He had some distinguished gray around his temples, while my hair had faded to gray nearly half a century ago.

My birthday party went off without a hitch. Our kids were all here for once. Katie, Elena, and their two had joined us. Faith, Trevor, Denis, Emory, and their children, too. Along with Xavior's parents. The house was full. They all drifted in and out of the estate for what seemed like weeks.

When it was finally us and our children, I delighted in the rare moments we were all together.

One morning, I listened to our three playing outside in the pool. We were staying in his upstairs apartment for the time being, and Xavior had left the glass doors to the bedroom open. It was larger than our cottage, and our whelps all had enough space to keep them from becoming territorial. The twins were nearly fifty, and Phil was barely into his thirties. They were all still babies by dragon standards.

I hadn't realized I had nodded off until I felt the bed move and arms wrap around my torso.

"Feeling tired this morning, love?"

"Yeah. Maybe you were right about the cough." As if to make a point, I made a gross hacking sound that was unproductive. It had been for a while. "Probably a cold or something."

"How about I have Dr. Babelin drop by this afternoon? He told us to call if your cough wasn't better by now."

"Sure. Sounds good." I patted his arm.

When James Babelin showed up, I managed to talk Xavior into leaving the apartment for five minutes to get me something.

"I'm tired, Doc. Don't sugarcoat it."

"It's time, Gregor."

I nodded. "Can you put things in motion? Call Jordan. He'll know what to do."

"You want me to tell him?" James meant Xavior. I shook my head.

"He already knows. He's only being stubborn about it. I'd be that way too if I were in his position. I'll tell him when he comes back."

As if on cue. "Tell me what?" Xavior's bright face made me smile, and I was pretty sure I was about to ruin everyone's summer.

"Can you call the twins and Phil? I want to talk to everyone." Xavior nodded and didn't ask why.

It wasn't too bad, though it was hard to breathe at times. That was normal, given my body was shutting down. I had meds to make it less painful, but they made me pretty loopy.

Xavior spent most of his time curled up next to me and only took a break when one of our whelps took his place.

"Xavior." I wasn't sure if I said his name right. I mumbled a lot more because of the meds.

"Right here, love."

I turned my head until I saw him. I narrowed my eyes. "You can't follow me."

"That's not your decision to make."

"Don't leave them. Not yet. They're too young." Tears pricked my eyes. Xavior's muscular arms rolled me toward him and held me tight.

"Jordan's here. I suspect that was your doing. I'm not happy about it."

"I don't care."

"You do, or you wouldn't have called him." He rocked us gently. It was soothing, and I almost slipped into a light doze.

I jerked slightly and opened my eyes, forcing myself to stay awake. The room was dim, which I appreciated. "One hundred."

"Five."

"Seventy-five."

This was an old argument-slash-game between us. I started it with him when I turned sixty-five. He had to promise me he'd stay alive after I died, and I wouldn't kiss him until we agreed on a number.

"Fifteen," he said with a whimper.

"Fifty-five." I rested my head on his shoulder. Our old argument was tiring me out.

"Thirty-five."

"Fifty, final—" I couldn't get enough breath just then. "Offer."

"Fine, fifty. You win. Don't go yet. Please. . ." Xavior begged, and I wished my body would have listened, but we kissed instead, and as far as endings to stories go, mine's not half bad.

I watched as Xavior hugged my body and cried. I took a solid breath and then another. Well, it wasn't a breath. I was dead, or at least I was pretty sure of it. There was a shimmering blue light beyond the door to our room. I followed it and saw the children asleep in chairs and on couches around the living area. I walked past them and followed the light into the hall, where I ran squarely into Edward.

"Shit."

"Indeed," Edward said.

"Wait, you can see me?"

"Yes, Greg. I can see you. Come this way, please."

"Where are we going, Edward?" The guy hadn't aged at all in the time I'd known him. The fact that he could see whatever I was now was definitely weird, but I trusted him, so I continued to follow him wherever we were heading.

"You'll see, Greg. I think you'll approve." Edward said.

"The last time you called me Greg, you kicked my ass at dancing. Do you remember that?"

"I do. That was a fun night." He walked down another hall in Xavior's estate to one I'd never seen before.

"What are you, Edward? I mean, I know it's rude to ask, but I'm dead, so I can't really tell anyone." I glanced around. The hallway we were in was long, with one doorway at the end.

"I'm a guardian, Greg." He gave me a faint smile. "Xavior will keep his promise. You'll have to find him again, but he'll wait for you. You need to hurry, though. Your opportunity is fleeting."

"What opportunity?"

"A second chance, and a longer go this time around." He pointed down the hall, and the door swung open. "But you need to go now, before it's too late."

I glanced at Edward, then at the door. It was slowly closing. I reached for Edward and hugged him. He was stiff as a board, but I didn't care. "Thank you."

I ran through the door before it closed.

Two individuals walked toward me, and by their smell, I knew one was a dragon and the other was fae. They were having a candid conversation when something familiar about the dragon's smell caught my attention. I shook it off and continued on my way, not giving it a second thought. It wasn't until there was a tap on my shoulder that I turned around and gazed into emerald green eyes.

"Excuse me, do I know you from somewhere?" The dragon said in Portuguese.

"I doubt it," I replied. Or, more accurately, the bracelets that read my hand movements replied in a preset feminine voice. As long as he spoke Portuguese, I could read his lips.

"You smell familiar," he said.

I scoffed. "That is the least flattering pickup line I've ever heard." I turned to go, shaking my head at his feeble attempt. "Goodbye."

He reached out to touch my arm before I turned away completely. "No, I'm sorry, wait. Please. We're visiting your city because my boyfriend here has a movie he's shooting a few blocks over. Would you like to see the production?"

"Xavior, she wants nothing to do with you. Leave it." The fae spoke Portuguese as well. Interesting.

"Give me a sec, Jordan." He turned back to me. "I can give you my information. If you want to come by, message me and I'll make sure you have the VIP tour."

"What for?" I gave him a curious look. This dragon was forward.

"You remind me of someone. That's all." He took a deep breath and shook his head as if remembering something. The light in his eyes dimmed slightly. "On second thought, I apologize. Sorry to bother you."

"Wait," I said. "Give me your information. My roommate would love to visit the movie set. She likes his pictures." I pointed at Jordan, his disguise more than obvious to me.

"You recognize me?" Jordan asked.

I nodded. "I know you're glamoured, but I have a knack for seeing past them."

"She's a dragon too, Jay."

"I know, Xavior. I'm not blind."

I smirked at them and shook my head. "Send me the information." I watched as Xavior made a gesture toward me and his information appeared on my retinal display.

"Can I ask your name?" Xavior's curiosity did not surprise me.

"Karina."

We all stood there awkwardly for a moment. "Good afternoon, gentlemen." They replied politely, and I continued on my way. *At least they were cute.* I was curious what my roommate might think about them, and somewhat curious about why a dragon was with a fae. There was a story there, I would bet anything.

RED & THE WOLF

M. L. EADEN

AUTHOR'S NOTE
RED & THE WOLF

This was an alternate universe story created for a Tapas event I was involved in, combined with several other authors. Often when I write these AUs, I usually figure out how to make them part of canon without making the actual events of the story part of the canon.

Until now, this story has been available as a free download when you join my newsletter. This will be the first time it is published wide.

Content Warnings: *on-page sex, death of a partner, grief, cannibalism.*

RED & THE WOLF

Xavior

I dropped into bed, exhausted from working at one of the larg-er were-creature festivals. Some of the different public safe-ty headquarters volunteered to help with security and crowd movement. It was three days of magic, music, and shifters of all kinds.

Most kinds, I should say. Werewolves tended to stay away from large gatherings like that. Greg hadn't ever volunteered for the festival before, but I had talked him into working a couple of shifts with me. He did pretty good, keeping his amazement in check, mostly. It made me laugh a little to see him so out of his element.

I closed my eyes, thinking about Greg, as seemed to be the case more and more these days. I often dreamed of him, but tonight I dreamed of my time wandering Europe, or so I thought.

The dirt road in front of me made it easy to put one foot in front of the other. The sun shone hot on the hood of my red traveling cloak. While the pack I wore wasn't nearly as full as it could be, it felt heavy on my back. I opted for a rest under a tree close to the road, opposite an open field being grazed by several animals. Once settled, I pulled out an apple, a bit of cheese, and my ever-reliable water flask.

The moment I took a sip of water, I heard a low growl from behind me. My scales vibrated under my skin, threatening a shift in response to whoever was there. Was someone actually trying to threaten me, or was I in their territory? Even so, most sentient individuals, whether shifters or *weres,* knew well enough not to engage a dragon. I untied my cloak and slipped it off my shoulders.

"You can be polite, or you can continue to growl. It makes no difference to me. Once I've finished eating, I'll be on my way."

They paced behind me and continued to make their presence known. When I heard two feet instead of four padded ones draw close, I reached for my walking stick in preparation for violence. They might have had a better chance as their wolf. It surprised me they would purposefully put themselves at a disadvantage.

"Are you here for long?" A soft, low-toned voice asked.

"No. Only passing through. I'm visiting my grandmother."

"Are you? Is she far from here?"

"Not very far. Another day or so."

"Why not fly? You have wings, don't you?"

"Walking lets me meet individuals and learn things. There is a time and place for flying." I heard them take a few more steps toward me. Turning my head, I saw a dark-haired individual and a pair of dark brown eyes staring at me.

"Are you hungry?" Their eyes grew wide. I could smell their anxiety from here and the slightly sour smell of desperation. "Come. I'll share what I have if you sit with me."

"Too close to the path. Too bright," they said.

"Oh?" I shrugged. It didn't bother me to move, as I wasn't scared of them. "In that case," I picked up my things and walked deeper into the forest. I didn't walk directly toward the wolf, as I didn't want to challenge their position, nor did I look them in the eye. As I settled under another tree farther off the road, I waited for them to follow.

Slowly, they crept from the shadows and settled in the small clearing across from me. They were far enough away that neither of us could reach the other without moving.

"Are you thirsty?" They looked half-starved and dirty. Their human form had matted, greasy hair on their head and between their legs. They crouched as if they were still in their wolf form.

I offered my flask, but they didn't move toward me to take it. Instead, I motioned to toss it to them and watched their eyes as I gauged where to throw it. I lobbed the clay flask with its cork in a soft arch toward them. They snatched the flask out of the air without looking at it.

They drank, then realized that the flask was magical and didn't run out of water, and then drank more as if they hadn't tasted anything so wonderful. "You might want to slow down unless you can tolerate that much water on an empty stomach."

They slowed and looked at me as they re-corked the flask. "Clever item," they said as they tossed the flask back toward me.

"Useful when traveling. Keeps me from having to follow streams and rivers."

"That wouldn't matter if you flew."

I shrugged. "Probably, but then, the journey is the mystery. It's the point, not the destination. As I said earlier."

They moved to lean against the tree nearest to them, and I heard their stomach rumble from across the clearing. I broke off a chunk of the cheese I had and tossed the handful to them. They caught that and smelled it. Their movement was tentative at first, as if they weren't sure it was real. When they inhaled, I could almost see the memories play across their face as they closed their eyes.

"My mate used to make something like this. It's been some time since I had something so pleasant." They took a bite and savored it. I didn't want to ask where their mate was. Something must have happened for them to be in this state and think a hunk of cheese was delightful fare.

"What's your name?" I kept my voice calm. They were more relaxed now that they were eating.

They chewed slowly and swallowed before they answered. "Gregor."

"Xavior," I replied. There was a nod of acknowledgement as he continued to eat. I watched as he finished the hunk of cheese, then drifted off to sleep. Most individuals would not have done that with someone they barely knew a stone's throw away. Especially one they knew was another predator. My concern for him grew as the day drifted away.

Gregor

I awoke with a radiant heat dancing over my skin from the soft glow of a fire not more than five paces from where I had fallen asleep against the tree. The dragon was still there. Reading, of all things. Of what, I had no idea. It had been a long time since I had seen a book, let alone written words.

"You didn't have to stay." I should have thanked him, but I didn't feel thankful. I was another few days, maybe a week, from death and had not hunted and barely drank anything, on purpose.

"No, I didn't, but I felt it was the better idea," he said.

After losing my mate, living without them seemed unbearable. I wanted a swift end. But he'd refused, then fed me, and even started a fire. In my weakened state, I'd given in to his kindness. "Why is that?" I asked, still groggy from sleep.

"Because. I am on a journey to learn. And I am hoping you will teach me."

"What could I possibly teach you?"

"You could tell me why you thought picking a fight with a dragon was a good idea."

"Who said it was a good idea?"

"Then why did you try it?"

"I thought you would kill me. We know dragons kill when provoked." Simple fact. Wolves stayed away from them. Tales of the dragon wars and their size meant they were no match for a human or a wolf.

"Who told you that?"

"Everyone knows that." I shrugged as if that explained my logic, and he laughed.

"Well, you're still alive, so wherever you heard such a thing, they're mistaken." He said, putting a marker in his book and closing it. "Though, if you had leapt at me, I would have defended myself."

"I didn't have the energy," I confessed. "When you offered me food, I hoped it was a trap."

"Poison, you mean?" Xavior asked.

"Or a more violent method. It does not matter to me." I took a breath and felt the weight of his gaze on me. I was still tired. The small fire was slowly sapping my will to stay awake.

"Why are you hungry for death?" His voice was soft with understanding and concern. It made me want to weep at the empathy he showed. It was a trait shared among a pack, or mates. He was neither and yet still kind.

"My mate is gone. A witch poached them and wears their skin as a false shifter. He visited our home to trade things. We had met him several times. I went to hunt for dinner, and when I came back, they were dead—skinned. The witch was gone. I tracked him until he disappeared. He used magic to hide his trail."

Xavior was quiet for a time. When he spoke, it jarred me out of my half-doze.

"It's possible my grandmother might know who they are. She's lived here for some time. If you have something of his, she might be able to figure out who this witch is and where he resides."

"You would do this for me?" His continued kindness astounded me.

"You deserve justice, and your mate deserves peace."

I looked across the clearing and saw the truth in his eyes. He was earnest in his desire to help me. His body language indicated that he had resigned himself to this effort. I almost refused his offer. But there was something about him that changed my mind.

"I accept your help."

"Good," he said as he pulled a blanket out of his bag. I wondered why until he got up and walked slowly toward me and handed me the blanket. "Tomorrow, we'll go to the stream near here and clean up. I can't have you visiting my grandmother in your current state. No offense. She would descale me." He smiled at his little joke. "Afterward, we'll set off to find your villain."

I took the blanket from his hand. He nodded and walked back to the other side of the clearing. I wrapped the cloth around me and felt an instant warmth and comfort that caused my throat to tighten as a held in a sob. It wasn't long before my effort to remain quiet drained me, and I closed my eyes, sleeping until daybreak.

Xavior

I spread the ashes and poured water on the fire before we walked to the stream. We were both quiet as we made our way to the water. When we arrived, I began to strip.

"What are you doing?" Gregor asked.

"Bathing. What do you think I'm doing?"

He looked at me and shook his head. He'd sat naked with me across from him all night, and suddenly he was shy of me being nude? It was somewhat hilarious, and I laughed a little as I removed the last of my clothing.

"Couldn't you bathe from the shore?" He was on the edge of the stream, crouched down, water lapping at his toes.

"No. It's better to get in. The stream isn't all that fast, and it's refreshing and quite enjoyable, I promise you." I opened my bag and removed a small piece of fragrant soap made with oil from a sage bush. It reminded me of my grandmother's home and the mix of smells that were inviting as much as they were protective. She practiced a kind of hedge magic. Even if it wasn't grandiose, it had power behind it.

I moved to the stream and stepped in. Steam wafted around me as my heated skin made contact with the water. I could feel the pleasant coolness caress me as I walked deeper into the flow. Gregor made a terrified sound from the shore as I sank into the water up to my neck.

It occurred to me he might not know how to swim. "My father taught me how to swim when I was a child. Water is dangerous to dragons, otherwise. You don't have to come into the water if you don't want to. I assure you I'm alright."

"You know how to swim?" His tone changed from surprise to amazement as he watched me move my arms and easily navigate the stream.

"Is that so strange?"

"Yes." He stood up and took a step or two into the water. He didn't seem to be bothered by the temp, only by how fast it was moving.

It was not that fast, really. I had to tread water some to keep my place, but even then, it wasn't that hard to do. I only had to take a few steps toward the shore to get my feet under me.

"Would you like me to teach you?" He looked at me and I smelled doubt, even with the running water around us. "If I were going to harm you, I would have done it last night while you were sleeping." I moved toward him, washing myself as I went. When I came near him, I tossed the soap up onto the shore and offered him my hands. "It's easy. I'll help you learn."

He took my hands, and we slowly waded out into the water. When we reached the drop-off, I expected him to kick his feet. Instead, he dropped like a stone below the surface. I swam down and grabbed him back up by his armpits. I turned him so his back was to me as I swam us back toward shallower waters. He sputtered and coughed up the water he had swallowed.

"Sorry about that. I should have told you to kick your feet. I thought you would do it naturally."

"You thought wrong, dragon."

That sounded like a kind of insult, but I let it go. He was shivering from the scare, and I picked up fear and anger from him. I put my feet down and let him float out in front of me. We stayed like that for a time, and he relaxed again.

"If you put your feet down, you can stand up."

He did, and I let him go. He turned to look at me. I went back to the shore and retrieved the sliver of soap, then returned and handed it to him. I floated near him to help if needed, but not so far that we couldn't talk.

"Thank you," he said. "You must be well-off to have such a luxury."

"Soap?" I forgot how uncommon it was in some areas. "My family makes it. We herd animals and tend farms around our estate. It has sage in it for protection. It also wards off illness. We often give it as gifts to tenants and visitors."

I tried not to watch as he used the soap on himself. Now that he was removing the caked-on grime, I noticed he was more than handsome. I closed my eyes to keep from staring, and the after-image of him washing himself in the morning sun caught my breath. When he cleared his throat, I opened my eyes.

He was next to me, holding the soap in his hand. I put my feet down and stood up. He was taller than me. Long-limbed and well muscled. I was glad the water was higher than our waists. An odd urge to kiss him bubbled up, and I tried to dispel it as I reached for the soap.

As my hand was about to clasp it, he moved, and I nearly fell into the water. I tried again, and he moved again. His scent changed to something playful, and maybe a little more. It made my heart beat faster. The game of keep-away was now in earnest as he switched hands and moved in the shallows away from me. It caused me to come closer to him as he kept moving the soap and I looked for other ways to grab it from him.

He turned his head toward me, laughing as he held the sliver of soap high above his head. I followed my instincts. Instead of reaching for it, I reached for his face and kissed him. His laughter stopped as he dropped the soap into the stream and reached for me, kissing me in return. Our kisses were urgent and passionate as I placed my hands on his hips to steady us as we offered up lips, tongue and teeth to each other.

He walked us back toward the shore, and I went willingly as we slipped over the rocks and moss there until we reached the higher bank where my pack and clothes were. Leaving him for a moment, I extracted the blanket and laid it out. He looked unsure about it until I sat down and offered my hand. He came to me willingly.

"You're warm," he said between kisses.

"Dragons tend to run hot. Is it not the same for wolves?"

"Only so much."

My hands roamed his body, caressing solid curves and defined muscles. When I reached his groin, the quiet moan that followed encouraged me. I moved my hand in a steady rhythm that had him panting in moments, and spilling his seed a few moments later. He clung to me as he caught his breath.

"I miss them."

I almost didn't catch what he said with his face pressed into my shoulder. When I felt his breath hitch and his scent turn to grief, I figured out who he meant. I wiped my hand on the blanket and brought him into a hug. He sobbed, and it nearly broke my heart.

When he quieted, I laid us down on the blanket next to each other and smoothed his hair from his handsome face.

"Do you think your grandmother will help me?" Gregor asked.

"I know she will, especially if I ask her. I'm her favorite grandson." He laughed a little as I offered him a smile. Some of the joy from earlier returned to his eyes.

"Then we should not delay our journey any longer. We'll need to return to my home. If we walk, it might take a week or more. I have followed the witch along the countryside for months. He stayed too close to the road and towns for me to do anything. That's when I lost his scent."

"We could fly."

"I thought you said you preferred to walk."

"I do, but in this case, I think we should make an exception. Can you read a map?"

Gregor nodded.

I worked out the route on the map to his home. It was a small cabin in the woods near the foot of a small ridge of mountains. If I could fly us to the area, he could get us the rest of the way within a few hours' walk. We agreed that the best way for me to carry him was for him to shift so his fur would protect him from the wind.

Gregor

I was curious about how Xavior planned to carry me when he dug into his pack and pulled out a large cloth with ropes attached to two handles.

"What is that?"

"An animal harness. We have to rescue animals from streams or remote areas sometimes. It's much easier to work with someone to get them into the harness and fly them back to their flock. Plus, the cloth will block the wind."

I thought twice about flying. "Maybe we should walk."

"Don't back out now. If we can get to your home in a day or so, I can take us directly to my grandmother's. We could have your villain within a week."

The possibility of avenging my mate spurred me on. I shifted as Xavior laid out the harness.

"Lie down here. When I pick up the handles, it will cradle you. Don't move too much or you'll start spinning and I'll have to land."

I nodded as I walked into the harness and lay down. Once he packed everything else and somehow made his pack disappear, he gave me the benefit of watching him shift. I hadn't realized how enormous dragons were. He was easily the size of a house. When he flapped his wings, the noise scared a whine out of me. In hindsight, picking a fight with a dragon was extremely foolhardy of me. He huffed out a breath and looked at me with his deep green eyes. Eventually, I settled, and I gave a small yip to let him know I was ready. Not that I was sure of this flying endeavor. But when he bent to pick up the handles with his mouth, there was no way to back out. Moments later we were aloft, with the rush of wind pushing him higher into the sky.

When we landed, I knew we were within a half day's walk from the cabin I used to call home. Even though months had passed, the trees near me still held the faint scent of mine and my mate's piss.

Xavior shifted faster than me, and I marveled at it before my shift distracted me. He was mostly dressed when I finished. I found myself disappointed I couldn't admire his body as I had when we bathed.

"It's this way." I pointed out the direction, and he nodded. We fell into step together, making good time. I could have run there in half the time, but I was unwilling to leave Xavior.

"Can I ask you a question? You don't have to answer if it's too unbearable." I knew then he wanted to ask about my mate. I nodded. Since he was helping me, it was only fair that I answer his questions.

"Why were you and your mate here by yourselves? Don't most wolves run in packs?"

"My mate was my beta. We had to establish our territory before we could start our own pack. We originally belonged to another pack about a day or so away on foot."

Xavior was quiet for a time. I realized I missed hearing his voice. "Why doesn't your grandmother live with the rest of your family?"

"Oh, well, she's feisty. Prefers to live alone, especially after my grandfather passed a few years ago. We all take turns visiting her every month or so to make sure she's okay, fix up her house, and tend to any other needs she might have. She's almost a thousand years old. My father is the youngest of three. My uncle lives far away and my aunt travels a lot, so it was left to our family to check on her."

I smiled. "She sounds like an amazing dragon."

"She's my favorite relative. I volunteer to visit her more often than not. I'll be sad when she passes. Thus far, visiting her has kept my wanderlust in check. I think my family won't take it well when I leave. Most of them are artists and craftspeople. They are used to working the land and staying close to home."

"Is something wrong that you seek to leave your family?" It perplexed me that someone would willingly leave everything they knew behind. Even when my mate and I moved ourselves here, we had each other, and we were only a day's travel from the pack. Far enough away to create a new territory, and close enough to visit.

"No, I love my family. They are absolutely wonderful. But my instincts and drive led me in a different direction than animal husbandry, or farming, or even painting, like my father. I crave the mysteries of life and travel. I want to learn new things, see new places, and speak languages that I've never heard."

We talked about our families and shared stories that made the path we traveled quicker. I hadn't realized we'd reached my home until I had entered the clearing and the smell of it hit my nose. It was familiar and rotten all at once. Death hung like a pallor, and it was evident from the lack of any activity around the house. No birds or mice. No squirrels. It was an eerie silence. I looked at Xavior and his face looked pinched with worry and concern.

"Stay here. I'll retrieve something we can use and then we can leave this place." He nodded and I moved toward the cabin. Memories flooded my senses as laughter and nights hunting together drifted like a river through my thoughts, along with quiet nights in each other's arms. It was a life thwarted by evil. Before I had been content to let myself die along with my mate, now I had found a purpose. Our meager collection of clothing was still in the chest where I'd left it. I selected my mate's favorite shirt, one I gifted to him over the winter solstice. To this I added a shirt and pants for myself, hoping Xavior could carry them in his pack. If I had to bathe to meet his grandmother, I assumed I'd have to dress to meet her as well.

When I came out of the house, I realized this place held nothing for me. I gave it one more look and turned from it toward Xavior. The sympathy I saw almost broke open the wound I had tried to ignore when he'd held me earlier.

"Are you ready?" he asked.

I looked back one more time and wished I could burn it down. Turning back to Xavior, I realized it might be possible. "Could I ask of you another favor?"

We watched as the cabin burned. Xavior's fire breath caught the wood alight easily. Xavior kept the flames from spreading to the surrounding woods with magical barriers. He was full of surprises. For a moment, it reminded me of the witch that I had trusted in my home and near my mate. I felt a sudden grief rise that I'd allowed the witch close enough to harm us, but that guilt died quickly knowing that I would find the witch and my mate would have justice. This dragon, whom I had hoped would end my life, instead put me on another path. If his grandmother was successful, I would owe them both my undying gratitude.

Xavior

Gregor slept as I flew us to my grandmother's house. When we landed in her nearby field, we used my flask and a cloth to wipe at our faces and bodies before we dressed.

"Do you not have any shoes?"

"Why would I wear shoes?"

"Sandals are quite comfortable, and it keeps shit off your feet."

"Or you could avoid stepping in shit." As I watched, he stepped over a pile of droppings without looking down.

"Okay, point taken." I laughed as we walked toward my grandmother's cottage. It was barely lit up with a hearth fire, which was unusual this close to dawn. My grandmother was an early riser. There were many mornings which she was already outside tending to animals and gathering her herbs. When we approached the door and no one stirred, I knew something was wrong. Gregor glanced at me as I reached out to knock. It took time, but I heard shuffling and eventually the door opened.

The stench that met us was unreal. I looked at the dragon in front of me, and I recognized her, but everything seemed off.

"Xavior! Come in darling, come in." She turned away from the door and moved toward the hearth. I couldn't bring myself to step over the threshold. I grabbed Gregor's arm.

"What's wrong?" Gregor whispered. Even though he asked, I could see the realization cross his face.

"That's not my grandmother," I replied in the same hushed tone.

"Why are you two waiting? Come inside, darlings. I'm making breakfast."

"Are you?" I moved to step inside and kept my hand on Gregor's arm. It could be that my grandmother was coming to her final moments, but I doubted it. Everything smelled wrong. "What's for breakfast, then?"

"Stew. Doesn't it smell wonderful?" My grandmother walked toward the cauldron over the fire and stirred it, which only made the stench in the house worse.

"When did you start eating meat?" My grandmother had eaten meat when she had to, but mostly fish. She preferred vegetables and fruits, along with whatever cheese she made. And honey. She loved honey. I glanced around her home. The crock of honey was spilled on the table, left to ooze its way onto the floor. "You've spilt your honey as well."

"Oh my, I should probably tidy that up. Could you be a dear and come inside and help me, Xavior?"

I didn't go inside, and I kept Gregor from entering the place as well. If they wanted us inside, they'd have to do more than tempt me with honey.

"Maybe you should come outside with us and take in the morning air. The sun is coming up," I offered.

"But what about breakfast? Isn't Gregor hungry?"

I glanced at Gregor, then back at the impostor. "How did you know his name? I didn't tell you."

"Clever, Xavior." The impostor laughed. "Your grandmother loved you best. I know more about you than any other in your family. When she died, she trapped me in this hovel. I think she did it to starve me. She didn't realize that I would be perfectly happy eating her carcass after I skinned her."

I felt Gregor tense. "You're the witch!"

"Yes. Foolish alpha. Your beta was no match for me. Now I have two skins. Easy enough to travel once Xavior releases me."

Gregor tore out of my hand and launched himself at the witch. I yelled to stop him, but he grabbed Gregor out of midair and tossed him toward a wall with no effort.

"You hurt him, and I won't help you. We can all die here." I took a step inside. I wouldn't leave Gregor alone inside the barrier. He needed my help.

"You don't have any leverage here, whelp. You'll do as you're told or I'll kill you both and eat you like I ate your grandmother."

I moved toward Gregor and checked to see if he was breathing. Once I knew he was alright, I turned toward the witch.

"You can drop the illusion."

The witch did so, and the stench from him was even worse. The skins he wore had maggots in them. I gagged from the smell, as if the sight of it wasn't bad enough.

"Release me from this hovel now. Or I'll make sure you're both cursed to bring me fresh skins for the rest of your days."

I'd die first, and I was pretty sure Gregor would too. "I'm not removing the magic. You're a corrupted creature, and you deserve to rot in this place."

The witch cackled. "Brave words from someone trapped as much as I am."

"Oh? You think so?" I picked up Gregor and walked toward the door. I had to trust that my grandmother had known what she was doing when she trapped the creature in her house.

I stepped over the threshold.

Gregor

I jolted awake. Disoriented at first, since I was at my parent's house in my old bedroom. I rubbed the crust out of my eyes and looked at the clock. I tried to dispel the vivid dream with a swipe across my face. It was about Xavior and wolves, and flesh-eating witches.

The shifter festival must have had more of an effect on me than I realized, but the dream seemed so real. I certainly wasn't a wolf, and Xavior looked so . . . young.

My phone buzzed on the nightstand next to me with a text from Xavior.

> Are you alright?

< Yes.

> Good.

< I had the weirdest dream.

> I know.

He knew? What the fuck? I called him.

Xavior answered with a groggy hello.

"What do you mean you know?"

"I can't explain what happened, but I think we were in the same dream," Xavior said.

"That was one fucked up dream, Xav."

"I know."

"Did any of that actually happen?"

"No, none of that happened. My grandmother died of natural causes. I met a wolf once and shared a meal. Everything else, I have no idea where that came from."

"Was it something we were exposed to at the festival?"

"Maybe. But we won't know for sure until we go back to sleep."

We didn't go back to sleep. We spent the rest of the early morning hours talking about the dream and details we both re-membered. I smelled breakfast cooking and remembered that my family had planned to spend the day on the water. It gave me an idea.

"My family rented a boat for the day. Do you want to come with us?"

"How soon are you leaving?" I heard him sit up in bed. The mental image brought a smile to my face.

"After breakfast in about an hour or two."

"I'll be there."

"Xavior," I hesitated.

"Yeah," he said.

"Even though that was a really weird dream, thank you for being there. And thank you for wanting to spend time with my family."

"I like your parents, Greg. And I like you a lot. I'd have your back no matter where we ended up. See you soon." He hung up without waiting for a reply.

I flopped back on my bed with a sigh. I had it pretty bad for that dragon.

GREGOR
&
XAVIOR

FIREBAUGH RESORT

Author's Note
Firebaugh Resort

Firebaugh Resort started as a way to focus my short story energy. Additionally, when writing the second volume of the Saint George Chronicles, there were all these lovely secondary characters that popped in and out of the story. I couldn't let them be one-offs.

I have many more stories planned around this resort and even a small novella series that I hope to work on, centered specifically on DracoCon, which is mentioned as one of the reasons the resort was built in the first place.

Of the two stories included here, one will be familiar to some readers and the second one might be new.

Calm Heart features some of the more unique scenes I've ever written. While it might not push the boundaries for some, others might find it slightly disturbing. Definitely check the content warnings.

And for those who are wondering, Felven will have their own story at some point. It's only a matter of when.

Content Warnings for Rare Temptations: *on-page sex, teratophilia, accidental attraction/stalking.*

Content Warnings for Calm Heart: *on-page sex, teratophilia, blood, implied sex work, depression, mental instability.*

About the Resort

Firebaugh Resort welcomes all magical species and their guests

The resort offers world-class accommodations, shopping, and amenities that specialize in the needs of magical species and magic users. The grounds offer many activities to delight guests, including a wide variety of pools and sunning areas.

As for nightlife, there are several clubs, and dance floors which cater to our guests' interests. From La Salsa-rita dance club to the rooftop gardens, to our exclusive kink club—The Playground, we'll help you find the exact atmosphere to help you relax while you're at the resort.

Our renowned spa offers accommodations for all sizes and types of species, with hours available for evening risers. Besides the spa, many dragons, other magical species, and their guests can seek the privacy and luxurious surroundings of Dragon's Cove.

Every ten years, Firebaugh Resort hosts DracoCon, the premiere dragon-only convention that brings dragons from all over the planet to socialize and play together. Our state-of-the-art territorial controls and guest way-finders make this convention an experience no matter whether you're attending for the first time or a returning attendee.

Here at Firebaugh Resort, we take pride in creating a safe, inclusive environment for all our guests to be themselves.
We look forward to your visit!

(Author's note: The Firebaugh Resort is a location within the Mythical Desires Universe)

RARE TEMPTATIONS

Dragon Shifter Sapphic Romance

M. L. EADEN

A Curious Curiosity

Francesca

"This application looks acceptable, but explain to me why you would like to transfer from the Garden Café to The Playground? You don't have any other experiences that would be applicable here other than your waitstaff position," Ms. Eilidh said.

This was my second summer working at Firebaugh Resort. The café had hired me back for the season, but I was restless with the routine of it. I liked the customers well enough, but simply put, I was bored. So I applied for a host role at The Playground. I'd heard rumors about a demi-goddess working at the resort, but I'd never met one until now. Ms. Eilidh, pronounced A-Lee, had golden hair elaborately braided in a quasi-crown, with a large fishbone braid draped over her shoulder. I wanted to undo it and put it back together just to count how many twists were in her hair.

"Ms. Morgan?"

Crap, not good. How had I become that distracted? So unlike me. "Yes, sorry. I was thinking." I stopped just short of lying because I was thinking, though not about what other experiences could apply to the situation. There were several informational texts and articles I'd read over the years, but claiming they were mine would also be a lie. I wasn't sure how to proceed.

"I understand the nature of the club." The desire to convince Ms. Eilidh that I could be helpful while I gained more first-hand knowledge was paramount, as the subject had intrigued me for a while. "I'm well read on the subject, both fiction and non-fiction, detailing the nature of how and what might occur in such a setting."

Ms. Eilidh smiled. "So you're a tourist."

"A what?" The term she used confused me. I certainly wasn't a tourist. I worked at the resort after all.

"You're interested in the topic, but you have no actual interest. For you, it would be research, observation, maybe even titillation, but you don't have a passion or desire motivating you."

Learning. Interesting comparison. Based on Ms. Eilidh's response, I took a different tactic. "I am fluent in ten languages and enjoy learning. I've heard that BDSM is a language unto itself. One of the body and mind. Therefore, I'm interested in learning more about it."

She tapped her painted ink-black nails on her desk. My application and resume were on the surface display. "Learning more, but not living it," Ms. Eilidh said. I watched her eyes scan my documents again and my imagination conjured up what it might feel like to have her light tan skin under my hands, and those manicured nails scratch down my skin even as one of her pampered fingers danced across the interactive screen in front of her. I followed my line of imagination to her face, which seemed to glow in the light, but her dark brown eyes were assessing me as she caught me staring. "Do you see something you like?"

The flush of embarrassment crept up my neck and into my cheeks as I looked down at my favorite pair of high-tops, scuffed but serviceable. I didn't look up, but I could see every detail of her in my mind. Eilidh's sheer blouse was paired with a corset vest that framed and accentuated her large breasts presented in a way that begged to be caressed and licked. Wait, no. What was happening here?

"Did you do something to me?" I looked up then, my mortification replaced with annoyance. My voice was thin with it. I didn't like whatever she did to make me feel like this. Not one bit.

"Ms. Morgan, I'm not sure what you mean? You were staring. I only asked a question." She seemed confused rather than annoyed. It was a curious response to my accusation.

"But you did something to me to make me stare."

Ms. Eilidh took a breath that visibly expanded her chest and let it out. I was staring again. She shook her head slowly. "Whatever's happening to you, at this moment, I am not actively doing anything to cause it. While I have abilities that can influence a human like you're suggesting, I've never had a physical effect on a dragon, in bipedal form or otherwise. Unless you are part human?"

"No," I answered, still confused at my sudden desire, but she smelled like the truth. So why did I feel attracted to her when no one ever seemed the least bit interesting to me? Uncle Greg withstanding, but that was more because he smelled familiar. I blamed that on Uncle Xavior.

Why was this different? Why now? I took a deep breath and smelled honey, wine, almonds, aloe, and vanilla. I took another, and there was a very distinct floral smell, something that tugged at my memories of something I read. Fertility. "You're a fertility goddess."

"Yes, partially, though my father was not."

"Do you know if he was human or not? Could he possibly have been a shifter?" The scent grew more potent as my nose parsed it out. If her father was a shifter, it wasn't one I was familiar with by smell.

She stood up abruptly, tense at first, then visibly relaxed. "No, I... I'm sorry, I don't feel comfortable answering any more of your questions. I think we'll conclude this interview. Good day, Ms. Morgan."

I'd upset her, and that hurt me, not just emotionally, but almost physically. Asking about her parentage was not a polite thing to do. My curiosity had won out over my more rational approach. I didn't want to hurt her, which was an odd response. Why did I even care?

I backed away from her desk, but I kept my eyes on her as I reached for the door. When I was on the other side, I closed it, then ran down the back hall that would carry me to a side exit, and then outside. I needed fresh air and to spread my wings.

UNSETTLED

The resort had housing nearby for staff. Long-term employees had bungalows, while the seasonal workers had apartments. It wasn't required to stay on the staff side of the resort, but it made it easier to commute to work. Plus, there were other benefits—like our own facilities, pools, laundry service, and cleaning services.

I had a bungalow that faced out toward the desert. The views were always spectacular, no matter what time of day. It had the added benefit of the illusion of privacy. I was one of the least private people on the resort, but some days I craved solitude. Tonight was no different.

The interview with Francesca Morgan rattled me. I didn't expect her to react as she had. Dragons were wonderful conversationalists and gifted orators. Her current manager noted this especially. There were stories of her recommending things, settling arguments, soothing fears not only with patrons but staff as well. She had leadership potential. If I could have ascertained whether she did it to amuse herself or actually help, I might have considered her for the club's staff. Someone who could take an active role in working with the patrons, swaying their emotions to fit the mood, and creating an indelible interaction between the performers and the audience would have been something to see.

I hadn't expected the questions about my background and her blatant staring and sniffing. With the resort catering to all beings magical and their partners, it was commonplace to adapt to situations or interactions that were cross-cultural and cross-species in nature. Ms. Morgan's behavior was baffling. Dragons took in a lot of sensory information through their noses. Many shifters did. However, most dragons kept that information to themselves or made subtle inquires. It was apparent that whatever she had smelled caused a reaction she couldn't control, and I'd never seen that happen to a dragon, even when they were high on mating pheromones. Nor had anyone ever asked about my parents, which was a story I preferred to keep to myself.

They trained all staff on the species that worked at or attended the resort. When any new species presented themselves, they updated us immediately about protocols and interactions, primarily for everyone's safety and more so for the guests. The last thing you wanted to do was open a vampire's room during the day, bother an ifrit while they were sleeping, or make loud noises around fae—unless the fae wanted loud noises, then that was a different story. The resort served its guests, and they adhered to a code of conduct while here. As a result, everybody was happy and offered a relaxing environment away from the human-centric world.

The resort had been my home for some time. My sanctuary away from staff and guests alike. My evenings off were rare, so when I had one, I indulged in a strong drink and put on my comfiest nightie. On my private porch, I lit a fire in my chiminea, then flopped on my outdoor loveseat with the romance novel I was in the middle of reading.

The evening breeze was perfect, and the fire made it more than comfortable. It was so relaxing. I must have dozed because sometime later, I woke up to something licking my face. With my eyes closed, I swiped at it, and whatever it was left only to return. The soft tickling nature of it finally caused me to open my eyes.

Ever wonder how your life might end? I've had a number of years longer than an average human, but when you have a dragon staring you in the face in the middle of the night, it makes you wonder if you've reached the end of the road, so to speak. Not that dragons had actually eaten anyone in centuries, that we knew of, but there was always a first time, maybe?

Adrenaline shot through me, and I had to remember my training. Dragons respond to fear, sudden movements, and have excellent eyesight in the dark. With that in mind, I tried to slow down my breathing so I could communicate.

"Hello. Are you aware that you're in a private area?" *Lee, seriously, that was that all you could muster?*

The dragon's head moved, and their eyes blinked as if they suddenly realized where they were. They took a step back, and I sat up and waited to see what they would do next. Though now that I didn't have a face full of dragon teeth, I could admire the individual in front of me.

The red and black dragon, which was approximately the size of an African elephant, had beautiful golden-brown eyes and a crown of spiked protrusions. Their eyes reminded me of someone, so I made a guess. "Ms. Morgan?"

She made a startled noise and leaped into the air, then was gone with a few beats of her wings. Something was clearly wrong, and I couldn't fathom what that might be. Whether it was brave or silly, I planned to find out. I grabbed my empty glass, shut down my holo book, put out the fire with a flick of my wrist, and headed inside.

After throwing on a pair of jeans, a cotton tee, a hoodie, and tennis shoes, I left my bungalow to head to the apartment block where Francesca lived. I remembered her apartment number from the paperwork.

Once I reached her apartment, it occurred to me that maybe she would like to be left alone. But licking someone and flying off deserved an explanation if she wasn't in distress. So I gathered up my courage and knocked.

I half expected her not to answer, but when she did, she reached for my hand and pulled me inside. I stood there in my least flattering outfit and practically had to put my eyes back in my head when I realized Francesca was still nude.

Dragons were comfortable with nudity; I knew that. Maybe she assumed because of my job, it would be alright. And usually, that would be true, but fuck, she was gorgeous, slightly taller than me, and had natural hair with curls that cascaded around her head. I might be a goddess by birth, but she looked like one in the low light of her apartment. With her golden-brown eyes that could mesmerize you and flawless, beautiful brown skin. She took my breath away.

"Ms. Eilidh. I'm sorry."

"For what?" Because my brain was scrambled and remembering why I'd come to her apartment was the last thing on my mind. "Oh, that. It's okay. I was worried about you, though. Are you alright?"

"I don't know." She moved to her couch and curled up on it. Her response gave me cause for concern, so I followed and sat next to her.

We didn't speak for a long time. I broke the silence when it looked like Francesca was too lost in her thoughts. "Is there someone I could contact to help you?"

"Oh, well, not really. I don't know what's happening to me, and it wouldn't be a good idea to involve other dragons until I do." The disconcerting nature of her tone and the frown on her face compelled me to offer what help I could.

"I'm familiar with some things regarding dragon senses. Would it help to describe it? I'm willing to help if I can."

She looked at me, then turned her gaze to the window. "At first, I thought it was another aging cycle. My first one was last year, and it's rare, if not impossible, to have two so close together. I didn't have this kind of response working and meeting people here last summer. Something about your smell makes me feel like I'm high on lust or a drug specifically tailored to make me desire someone. Does that make sense? It's distracting and pleasant, and I find myself drawn to it because desire and lust are very unfamiliar sensations for me." Her gaze found mine.

While I had clients describe our sessions as a kind of high, or causing a similar response to a drug—because pain and pleasure can do that—I've never caused that response indirectly that I knew of, until now. "Would it be better if I left?"

"Probably, but I don't want you to." She moved, and I watched, feeling like a mouse. It was an odd sensation. No one ever made me feel like I was small. I'm not a small woman. My eyelashes were the only thin part of me, and I wore a glamor to fix that. But I wasn't wearing my tradecraft now. Nor was I dressed to meet clients or help with the club. I was me, un-adorned and completely vulnerable to whatever the dragon in front of me did next.

Which was to kiss me.

Her fingers traced my face and caressed my cheeks as our lips pressed together. I bit off a moan in response to one of the most familiar but gentle touches I'd received from anyone. It felt as if she had memorized my contours before she'd ever laid a finger on me.

My delight threatened to outweigh the gravity of the moment. She had just admitted that I was affecting her. The back of my mind screamed two things: Oh gods and goddesses, she's absolutely ambrosia. Also, stop her and talk now.

She drew back for a breath and immediately gave me another quick kiss, humming her pleasure into my lips. I barely got her name out of my mouth before our lips crashed together again and her tongue sought mine. Teasing in the most tantalizing way, promising a talent that might be applied beyond kissing. It appeared that's exactly what Francesca had in mind as she pulled at my hoodie and unzipped it. The soft fabric clung to my arms as I dragged myself away from her lips and panted out the most rational thing I could think to say. "Wait, wait. We should talk."

She blinked and licked her lips as her hands curled into the fabric of my jacket. "Aren't you attracted to me?"

"I am. Very." There should have been more to that, but I couldn't think of why at that moment. Were we both affected now?

"Good," Francesca said as her hands pushed the material off my arms while her lips never left mine. As she teased and caressed with her tongue and mouth, her hands fondled my breasts with feather-light touches and gentle pinches to my nipples. A moan escaped my lips, and she pulled back a little to meet my gaze and give me a sultry smile. "Do you like that?"

My breasts were sensitive, so anything felt nice, but she moved her hands in a way that tightened everything from my chest to my clit. "Yes," I breathed out as she continued her gentle onslaught. As my desire rose to meet hers, my willingness to be passive vanished. All I needed was her permission. "Can I touch you?"

"Of course, please." The small plea, the wanton plea. Fuck, I didn't know how many times I've heard that in my life while someone was under me, taking my paddle to their ass or kissing my boot, but that small surrender always motivated me.

My lips found hers again, and this time I gave her a preview of what was to come as my tongue danced with hers and teased around the edges of her lips. My hands caressed her sides and traced her modest breasts as I guided her toward the end of her couch, opening her legs wider, nudging her into position while I dropped to the floor to kneel in front of her.

Once I pulled away from her lips, her legs were over my shoulders, and I kissed down her torso to soft, punctuated moans with each kiss and lick I gave. I loved her responsiveness. It was heady, and I became needy for it.

I looked up at her, only a centimeter or two from her hair-covered sex. The curls on her mons appeared soft and delicate, which gave a pretty picture to the smell of her arousal. I was desperate for a taste of her and stopped long enough to ask permission. "May I?"

She nodded, but I needed her to say it. I wanted her to know that whatever happened next; we wanted this, and she had a choice. "Tell me what you want, Francesca." I put the tiniest bit of command behind my voice, and I got a soft growl in response with a slight glow in her eyes.

Her fingers reached for the simple binding that held my hair back and removed it, then she grasped my hair and gently yanked. My gaze met hers, eyes glowing with desire. "First, it's Freddie; second, I want your tongue on me... please."

"Well, Freddie, since you said please." We smiled at each other, then I magicked a quick barrier spell over my mouth before I continued. The spell was a simple technique to manage fluid exchange, which was very useful in my line of work.

I started with my tongue and explored her soft curls and folds until I found her clit. But I left it alone, which earned me a frustrated sigh from my partner. I wanted to discover Freddie's other spots before she came for me. I teased her engorged labia with quick touches of the tip of my tongue and long licks that traced her heated flesh. She sighed, then laughed or moaned in turns.

Her range of expressions was beautiful, and it urged me on. I drove my tongue into her, and she gasped from the invasion as I fucked her with it. Her hand tightened in my hair, and I knew I was somewhere between pushing her over the edge or teasing her too much.

When I lapped my tongue back to Freddie's clit, she writhed under my hands. Her legs kicked at my back, and her hands spasmed in my hair. I'd found her sweet spot just left of center and went at it for all it was worth. Her screams, gasps, and growls punctuated everything as she came for me.

"Oh, fuck. Oh, please, oh, fuck. Don't stop." I wouldn't dream of it. "I'm coming, oh fuck I'm coming!"

Whatever I thought might happen did not meet the reality of it. I've had woman's cum on my hands, body, and mouth. Sometimes it's a little; other times, it's a flood. What I didn't expect was both semen and vaginal fluid simultaneously. At least not in this situation. Or so I thought. I was willing to be wrong.

I didn't let up, continuing to make her ride the high I started for her until she pulled my head away amid her third orgasm.

She panted as I eased her legs down from my shoulders. Her couch and my shirt were completely wet, but I left those things for the moment. A quick cleaning spell solved a lot, but I was concerned about the dragon in front of me. Her eyes were heavy-lidded as I leaned up and kissed her gently. "Do you feel better, Freddie?" There was a grin and a nod. I didn't force more of an answer. "Come on, sweetie, let me help you clean up and put you somewhere proper to sleep." She let me pull her up from the couch, take her to the bathroom, and clean her up with a washcloth. Together, we worked out how to wrap her hair up to protect it. She was still tipsy on lust when I helped her to bed and pulled the covers up around her.

"Find me tomorrow. We should talk," Freddie said.

That sounded like a splendid idea. "I will, I promise." Then leaned over her to kiss her forehead and caress her cheek.

She smiled and promptly fell asleep, and within moments was making the cutest snoring sounds.

My quiet walk home had me thinking. Was this a one-off, or would Freddie need more help? It seemed to be a biochemical response, or maybe a magically influenced biochemical reaction? Dragons had sensitive noses. There were all kinds of talented physicians here. Maybe tomorrow I could talk with her about seeing one of them if it wasn't something natural.

There were so many questions, and Freddie might know some of the answers. Even if she did, the big question in my head was, what's next?

HOT MESS

FRANCESCA

I found her sitting at a table, reading something while she sipped her tea. Ms. Eilidh was perfectly composed for her day, and I was wearing my café uniform. Summer had come to the resort, and it was still cold in the mornings, but that didn't bother me much.

I nabbed three breakfast sandwiches and some coffee with a lot of cream and sugar, then made my way over to her.

"Morning, Ms. Eilidh. May I join you?" Her dark brown eyes lit up, and that made me smile.

"Please. And call me Eilidh." She pointed to the chair across from her. "How are you doing this morning?"

"Better," I said as I took a seat, admiring the grace and poise of the demi-goddess across from me. "How are you?"

"Adequate for a Wednesday morning. It will be a long day with a later night as the club prepares for the rest of the week."

"Makes sense to me," I responded. I couldn't hold back my excitement any longer. I desperately wanted to talk about what happened, and I hoped she didn't think I was being rude bringing it up over breakfast. "Last night was intense."

There was an amused look on her face. "Only intense?"

"Amazing, actually. I can say that I've experienced nothing like it."

Her cup stopped in midair as concern appeared on her face. "Wait. What do you mean by that? Are you saying you've never had such a night with someone before, or that you've never, ever done anything like it?"

"I mean the latter. That's the first time I've ever done anything sexual. I've never been interested in anyone enough to be sexual with someone. It seemed pointless unless it was my mate."

"But I'm not your mate." The lift of her eyebrow was curious, though she was still amused somewhat.

"I know, which is why this is so odd. The attraction I feel for you is overwhelming. Like someone flipped my lust switch." I chuckled, trying to lighten the mood.

We dragons were naturally curious and liked to experiment, which is why most of us were omnisexual. How else would we find a mate? Except I wasn't most dragons. I was something different, which is why my family was worried, I think. They would be perfectly fine with me being different. I knew my parents loved me, but it meant that it would be harder for them to help me. Though I knew my daddy, Gavin, would research the ends of the earth to figure it out. While my da, Brice, would cook, brood and do his best to keep everyone that came within the sphere of his kitchen fed so they could help find answers. It's also the reason I needed to leave their house. Granma-ma Faith was worried too. Truth be told, I wanted to leave home, but I didn't know how. Moving from Wales to Spain was a start. When Papa Ransford, my great grand-papa, suggested the resort, it seemed like a good idea at the time. So much so I signed up for a second season, much to my family's delight. Now, I wasn't so sure returning to work here was a good idea, considering what happened with Eilidh last night.

She set down her teacup. I took that moment to take a bite of my breakfast as she glanced away and then back at me.

"How would you like to proceed?" It was a calm, astute question that I hadn't thought about. Coming from the realms that Eilidh worked in daily, it sounded like a familiar beginning based on what I knew of how individuals would discuss needs, wants, and boundaries.

"Are we discussing the parameters of a relationship?"

"If you like." She picked up her cup and took another sip while I considered my options.

"Would we date or only have sex?"

"I'm not opposed to either or both. Would you like to date?"

"It would be a new experience." I thought for a moment. "I read a lot about it, but I've never dated anyone—"

"—Because you didn't see the need," we said simultaneously as I nodded.

"I'm starting to understand our circumstances. So, dating and sex. Is there anything else?"

Some non-fiction books talked about different types of relationships and boundaries. None of the fantasy books I'd ever read had relationships begin like this. There were so many tropes and types of meet-cutes that I was slightly disappointed this wasn't more natural. Though I was willing to put that aside for the sake of the experience. "No, I think I'm satisfied. What about you?"

"Me?" she asked. I was surprised she hadn't asked for anything. Though maybe she wanted to give herself some separation between what we were doing and her work life. Lucky for me, I enjoyed asking exactly those kinds of questions.

"Yes. A relationship has two sides, doesn't it? What would you like in return for dating and having sex with me?"

Her lips twitched slightly. She took another sip, then answered my question with a question. "How about information?"

"What kind of information?" I wasn't sure what she had in mind, but an information exchange wouldn't be out of the realm of a normal dating relationship. Communication was key, or so I've read.

"Any information you are willing to provide or give when I ask a question."

"That sounds reasonable. And I have the option not to give you the information."

"You do." She smiled. "Consider that I'd like to learn about dragons as much as you would like to learn about dating and sex."

"Oh. Is that all?" That seemed a little too easy from where I stood, but maybe she was curious, too.

She shrugged and smiled. "For now."

"I find that acceptable." I wiped my hand on a napkin and held it out to Eilidh. She took it, and we shook on it.

"I was thinking. The first thing we could try is a romantic dinner. Thoughts?" Eilidh asked.

A romantic dinner will be so easy. I totally had this. My da would be so proud when he found out that all his kitchen instructions didn't go to waste. "Do you have any allergies?"

"No."

"Anything you dislike?"

"Not particularly."

"Anything you do like?"

"Strawberries."

Noted. "What time would you like to meet tonight?"

"Let's say eight. I'll have an hour where the club will be fine without me."

"Eight o'clock. Sounds good." Plenty of time to plan. I was already making mental calculations on what I had time to prepare when she asked a question I wasn't expecting.

"Should I take contraceptive precautions?" She finished the last of her tea while she waited for my answer.

I blinked. *Oh, shit. Right.* I was so used to my dual nature that I somewhat forgot that I could, in theory, make someone pregnant. Much more likely as a dragon, but less likely as a biped. But less didn't mean zero. "Yes. That's a good idea."

"Very well, then. I'll be at the club, so whenever you're ready, you can find me there." She stood and then pushed in her chair, picking up her teacup and plate. "Have a good day, Freddie."

"You too, Eilidh. See you tonight." We smiled at each other as Eilidh left me with a lot of curiosity and the rest of my breakfast.

DINNER FOR TWO

FRANCESCA

This wasn't so hard. I don't know what everyone makes a fuss about. 'A little goes a long way,' and 'making the thought count' were platitudes I knew of but didn't put into practice until today.

I had the table set up in her office while Eilidh was out making rounds. One chicken strawberry salad with strawberry shortcake for dessert. One candle for romantic ambiance and a bottle of the house red wine to pair with everything. Nothing over the top. Perfectly metered out for a first romantic dinner.

As the click of her heels down the hall announced her approach, I lit the long, tapered candle and waited for her to enter. The door swung open with a quick motion, and Eilidh stopped unexpectedly as she noticed the table and her office.

"Am I late?"

"No. I'm a bit early. But I wanted to make sure we could spend the hour you have together."

"That's thoughtful." She moved around the table and me, and went to her desk. She put down the riding crop and took off her leather gloves. After that, she was like a different person. Her shoulders relaxed, and she smiled.

"So, what's for dinner?" She said as she came toward me. I pulled out a chair and prompted her to sit, which she did. Then I took my seat.

"A simple shredded chicken and strawberry salad with feta cheese and mixed greens, along with the house red wine. And a strawberry shortcake for dessert. Which I placed in your mini cooling unit until we're ready." She looked impressed, which pleased me.

She pointed to the serving tongs. "This looks delightful. May I?" I held up my plate while she piled half of the salad mixture on mine and then put the rest on hers.

I picked up the wine and poured it. "Say when." She watched with her beautiful dark eyes and waved off when the glass was a third full. I poured a half-glass for myself and started to eat dinner.

"How was your day?"

"Remarkably pleasant. I had two clients who set up some couple play, another who wanted a demonstration of various techniques and toys for anal play, and the last was a floor show for the club."

"What kind of floor show was it?" I took a bite, waiting for her next words. Half the reason I applied was because of her work in the club. With this arrangement, I wouldn't have to work in the club, but I'd still garner information.

"Mostly soft discipline. Spankings with the crop when they do something I like or don't like. One host usually volunteers to be spanked. It's not a full scene, but something like an appetizer."

"To put people in the mood."

"Yes, precisely." She took another bite of the salad. "This is amazing. Did you make it?"

I nodded. "The café has a kitchen, so I borrowed it and sourced the ingredients from them as well."

"They must trust you to let you cook during off-hours."

"Well, that's mostly borrowed trust. One of my parents is Brice Morgan."

Eilidh blinked. "The Brice Morgan, the Michelin-star chef from Wales?"

"Yes?" Was Eilidh another fan of my father's cooking? I was proud of his reputation, but personally, I liked it better when he was just 'Da' and made me a bowl of oatmeal.

"I've eaten at Catch Your Peacock."

I was always curious about people who visited my da's place. He put a lot of passion into his food. "What did you eat?"

"Smoked cured lamb with roasted leeks, and a slice of fresh Bara brith with vanilla ice cream and black tea sprinkled on top." The awe in her voice was lovely, and I held out the bottle of wine to see if she wanted more, and she nodded while I poured. "How did he come up with the name of the place?"

"Not sure. I never asked. But Da has cooked as long as I've known him, maybe longer. He's almost three hundred years old, while Daddy is two-fifty-five or two-sixty, I forget."

"You sound like you get along with your parents."

"I do. They care a lot. I'm their only offspring so far, so they've been protective. I'm sure it will wear off once they have another whelp."

Her face was slightly pinched even though she smiled, and her scent was... and that's when I realized I had made a mistake. One sniff and the lust monster in me rose from the fog. Maybe I should have given myself some kind of scent blocker. My arm twitched, and I almost knocked over the bottle of wine.

Eilidh glanced at me, and I tried to play it off as nervousness, which wasn't that far from the truth. "Um, so, I know you're busy." I stood. "I'll let you finish dinner. And, um, the dessert is in the fridge. If you like, you can call me after you're off work, okay?"

"Freddie, what's wrong?" Her gaze tracked my movement toward the door as she put down her napkin.

I tapped my nose. "You, um, smell better than dinner."

"Oh?" She blinked, then her eyes narrowed. "I do?" Her lips curved into a sultry smile as she stood and moved toward me. I made flailing hand gestures to ward off the ideas I could see forming in her eyes. She took a step in my direction, and I put a hand on the door.

"Eilidh, just. . . please. . ."

"Please, what?"

Rendered nearly speechless, I couldn't tell her I thought it was a bad idea for her to come any closer. I wanted more of what she'd done to me last night, and I wanted to do things to her. Things I'd long conjured in my imagination or read about, but never had a participant before now.

"Don't you need to be back at the club in. . ." I glanced around for any time reference and noticed it was only eight-twenty. "In like forty minutes? Wouldn't you like to finish dinner?"

"It's not my fault you added another course." She came closer, and I stood stock-still. The space between us shrank until all I could see were her eyes. "Breathe, Freddie." She touched my face gently, and I relaxed slightly. "What are you scared of?"

There were so many things that went through my head. I hadn't thought I was scared, but maybe I was, if only because this was all strange and triggered by her smell. What if it was something addictive, and I turned into this needy, wanton dragon that constantly desired her touch? What if I hurt her? What if my mate came along and I didn't know it because I was with her, and then I didn't want to leave her? What if. . . what if. . . what if?

Amid my spiraling, Eilidh somehow had me crouch down and put my head between my knees. Her hand caressed my back as the persistent scent that triggered all this soothed me.

"Feel better?" she asked in a quiet voice.

I glanced up, then uncurled slightly to lean back against the door. "How did you know?"

"That you were having a panic attack? I've had enough clients to recognize when they are on board with what's happening or freaking out. Do you want to talk about it?"

She sat down next to me in a cross-legged pose that framed all of her, and my brain wanted to hang onto that image along with the beauty and peace it conveyed. I also wanted to crawl into her lap and lick every inch of her. I laughed out loud at my dichotomy of thoughts. After a few moments, she tittered with me, to which I laughed more. Her giggle was adorable.

"I apologize for ruining dinner."

She smiled and reached out, offering her hand to me. I took it. "You did nothing of the sort." She stood, then pulled me up with her. "How about I walk you home?"

"I'd like that, but what about the club?"

"I manage this place; it doesn't manage me."

On our way out, she asked Javier to supervise in her absence. I held her hand all the way home. When we arrived at my apartment, I placed my thumb on the fingerprint reader, and the door opened. Unwilling to say goodnight so soon, I gently pulled her inside.

"Do you need anything else?" Eilidh asked as she reached up and brushed some strands of hair behind my ear.

You. Before the thought finished flashing through my mind, I pressed my lips to hers, and Eilidh melted into the kiss as if she had waited for me to give in or figure myself out. I tried not to think about it as we moved to my bedroom, and clothes quickly found themselves in other places.

I growled softly as her ass hit the bed. I kissed my way down from her lips to her neck until I reached her voluptuous breasts. Her hands were reassuring as she caressed my back and shoulders while I made her moan from gentle sucks and kisses to her nipples and chest. I continued on, my hands caressing her sides and belly. She was a treasure of soft roundness that reminded me of a warm pillow. I licked her navel. She giggled—that soft giggle that was almost girlish—as I moved lower.

My gaze stopped on a mark that she had on the inside of her right thigh. It was three s-shaped spirals woven together to form a triangle with curves. It had hash marks in the middle of each spiral. My curiosity got the better of me. "What's this?"

"Oh, that's our protection." Trust a demi-goddess of fertility to know about contraception. I kissed the mark, amused and relieved that she had taken the precaution. I then tilted my head until I could blow a gentle breath across her mons and urged her legs wider while I marveled at the wild bush between them.

"You're beautiful," I said as a glanced up, meeting her lustful gaze.

"Your eyes are glowing," she said in a breathy voice.

I looked down. "May I?" I had learned from Eilidh. Willingness didn't always equal consent. I liked that she asked me, and I wanted to do the same.

"Yes," she said, her voice still breathy. "Please." I kissed the very top of her slit, and she moaned. She surprised me because I hadn't really done anything yet.

"Are you encouraging me or being nice?"

She sat up slightly, elbows pressed to the mattress, and glared at me. "Are you nervous or being a tease?"

My gaze locked with hers, and I purposefully watched her face as I spelled a magical protective barrier over my mouth, then pressed the tip of my tongue through her golden-colored curls to settle it right next to her clit. When I applied the gentlest of flicks, barely a tap, the gasp that followed set me in motion. I sucked, teased, licked, and lapped at every inch of her. Once I had the lay of the land, I pressed two fingers into the center of her wetness and focused on her clit with my tongue.

Eilidh bucked and writhed under my attention. "Fuck, like that. Just like that. A little more to the right. . ." I complied as she thrust her hips onto my fingers, and I flicked my tongue. "I'm close, so close," she panted. "When I tell you to move, move."

I wanted to ask where she thought I should go when she screamed into her orgasm and barely yelled before a torrent of liquid shot from her. It landed on my shoulder as I moved my head in time, but she continued to squirt a few moments more while my fingers stayed pressed to her g-spot.

"I've read about this." It fascinated me. My lust for her rose tenfold now that her smell and juices were all over me. I moved up onto the bed next to her as she panted and shivered through her orgasm. She moaned when I moved my fingers as I repositioned myself.

"Wait. . ."

My hand went to her stomach, and I pistoned my fingers into her, adding a third with ease as she groaned and threw her head back on the bed. "Come for me again." This time, I knew what to expect.

"Oh, fuck, more. . . Freddie, please."

It's heady knowing you've reduced a goddess to begging. I added another finger and pressed my thumb to her clit near the right spot so that the motion of my hand would play into the sensitivity I knew she was feeling. She screamed for me again as she orgasmed, and I was elated. I bent my head down to lap at her wetness as her hand settled on my neck.

"More?" I glanced up at her. I wanted more. Truth be told, I wanted everything. Every sexual thought I'd ever conjured, I wanted to explore. Previously, I had wondered about these things in a more clinical fashion. Interested but not titillated, or even excited. But now, possibilities opened up, and my imagination saw no bounds between two consenting adults.

Eilidh nodded, and I continued until she reached for my arm to still it. I let her come down a little before I slipped my fingers from her. As we lay together on the bed, I took in the flushed, soft curves of her face, the rise and fall of her voluptuous chest, and the sweat-laced curls along her scalp and neck.

The gentle snore from her threatened to make me giggle. "Eilidh," I breathed. "We should clean up."

She lifted her hand, and a moment later, the sheets under us were dry, and my hair was in a bonnet.

"Okay, clever goddess, move so we can snuggle properly." She giggled, and the sound etched itself on my heart.

Once we were finally ensconced together in my bed, her back to me, my arm draped over her waist, caressing her belly, I breathed in her scent. It was everything I expected, but one particular note was missing or muted. I hadn't realized I'd buried my nose in her neck and hair until she giggled again.

"That tickles."

"Apologies, Eilidh. Your scent is pleasant, but I noticed it smells different after sex."

"Oh, is that bad?"

"No," I rushed to say. "Just intriguing."

"Mmm hmm," she replied before I heard her soft snores again.

CONTINUED EDUCATION

Eilidh

Freddie and I continued to meet up for dinner, or a movie, or to binge-watch the latest holos. She loved telenovelas, and we'd often slip into discussing them in Spanish. Sometimes, my translation spell didn't work as well as if I knew the language. When it fucked up, she would laugh and let me know why.

One night, after a rather vigorous fingering session, I broached the subject of what else she'd like to try.

"Everything!" Her excitement was charming, and we laughed at her exuberance.

"Everything is a long list. What would you like to try next?"

"Oh, that's a good question. I have a lot of ideas." I didn't prompt her and waited. My hand caressed her thigh to let her know she was in a safe place without speaking into the silence.

"If I were approaching this with some kind of scientific rigor, I would seek someone out with a penis to decide if I enjoyed that or not."

I smiled. "What about an excellent facsimile?"

"Oh? AH! Yes, I suppose that might be alright. Approaching someone to see if they wished to experiment with copulating could be daunting."

There was a topic that I thought would be important to ask, but I had to admit that I enjoyed our time together too much to ruin it with questions. Now seemed as likely a moment as any since Freddie brought up other genitalia.

"Have you ever thought about who you might be attracted to?"

"Not particularly. Dragons are sequential hermaphrodites, and mates can come in all sexes, shapes, and sizes. If it were another dragon, their bipedal form wouldn't be important. Most dragons are attracted to nearly everyone, or can be."

She left out an important part of that statement. "I sense that 'most' does not include you. Would you agree with that?"

Freddie looked away at first, then caught my gaze. "I never saw the need or the desire. If the knowledge I obtained from books and my experience were a mate, I'd long ago have declared my choice and ensconced myself in whatever place they resided." So if there was a sentient library in the world, Freddie would likely mate with it on the spot. Noted.

"Are you concerned about what we're doing?" Lust and attraction usually went hand in hand. So it interested me that one did not lead to the other for her. If Freddie only felt lust, I knew I needed to keep my own feelings in check.

"No, I enjoy our time together. It's been eye-opening for me."

I tried to keep the concern off my face, but dragons had a keen sense of smell, especially for emotions.

"You're worried. Why?"

"I feel like I'm influencing you and your choices, even inadvertently, because of something about how I smell."

"But you don't smell that way now."

"I don't?"

She shook her head. "Actually, you lose whatever scent I'm drawn to after an initial coupling. It might relate to a change in endorphins along with pheromones, but I'm not completely sure. I would need to take pre and post-colitis samples to know."

"Freddie," I said in a teasing tone. She grinned. The tangents were one thing I adored about her.

"Simply put, Lee, I haven't continued dating you for that reason alone." She reached up to brush some strands of hair out of my face. "You're fun, understanding, and our sexual activities are extremely enjoyable."

"Why do I sense a clause to that statement?"

"I'm leaving in a month."

The soft drift into sleep was utterly destroyed by that information. I sat up, and Freddie came with me. I tried to say something, anything, but eventually landed on, "that's good to know."

"Lee," she said with a sigh in her voice. She knew before I did. I was disappointed and maybe even a little crushed. Damn dragons anyway, practically empaths because of their noses. I extracted myself from the bed, threw on a robe, and went to make tea. I couldn't continue this conversation without something warm to soothe my nerves.

As I made two cups of chamomile tea, I wondered how I'd become attached so quickly. There was no commitment between us. No promise. Only an agreement of sorts. I liked Freddie. She was fun, quick to try things, caring and thoughtful. The sex was amazing, and that was saying something given my work and other opportunities I'd had in my long life.

I noticed Freddie had thrown on a T-shirt, and nothing else as she walked into the kitchen. She hopped onto the counter and picked up the other cup I'd made. I watched as she took a deep breath and smiled.

"When Daddy would spend the whole day with his research, Da would make chamomile tea with honey and whiskey to coax him into taking a break." She took a tentative sip. "It was like magic. Daddy would drink the tea, and within a few minutes, he would stop what he was doing and ask about everyone else's day, then help put me to bed. I'd listen to them as they wandered to their bedroom, giving each other kisses."

"Your parents sound wonderful."

"I don't think I could ask for better." She took another sip as I watched. "I'm sorry I didn't tell you sooner, Lee. I should have."

I shrugged. "Most of the work here is seasonal. There are very few of us who stay on permanently. It shouldn't have surprised me." But it had, and what's worse, were the sprouts of feelings I had now. As much as I had wanted to keep them in check, they had grown like wildflowers where I least expected them.

"What would you like to do?" Freddie put down her teacup, folded her hands, and leaned over enough to put her elbows on her knees and her chin in her hands.

"How old are you, by the way?" I was avoiding the question. She knew it because she unfolded herself and looked pensive.

"I'm eighty-nine. What about you?"

"Ninety-two! You look amazing for your age."

She threw back her head and laughed. If it wasn't for her bonnet, her hair would have adorably spilled around her head. "You are quite the fox yourself, Eilidh. I wouldn't have guessed you were older than me."

"Benefits of being a demi-goddess. We have a shelf life, but it's much longer than most humans."

"Noted," said Freddie with a grin. "The oldest dragon I know is Grand-papa Ransford. He's almost six hundred years old, I think. I only know that because I saw some of my daddy's documents on our family tree."

I took a breath and thought about the oldest being I knew, and that was a tough call. "I think it's Felven, the concierge. But that's only based on some things they said one night, and the way they phrased it was something like, 'In all the thousands of years this planet has turned, and my eyes have seen, there has been none more beautiful than you.' But it could have been a line since they had me trussed up in their tentacles like a fly in a spiderweb."

Freddie blinked. "Are you saying you've had intercourse with Felven?"

"They're extremely talented with their many appendages. They feed off the magical energy around the resort most of the time. But occasionally, they like to create some of their own." I finished my tea and set the cup down.

"Sounds like you made an impression on each other."

"You're wondering why we aren't dating?" Freddie nodded. "They have no concept of it. We've shared each other a few times over the years that we've worked here. They have no need for a companion beyond occasional interactions, especially since they reproduce asexually. At least that's what they explained to me."

"Oh." Freddie looked down. I could see her piecing the puzzle together. When she looked at me, I expected her to ask a question. Almost everyone asked, 'why was I single?' but I cut her off instead.

"Listen, don't feel bad, okay? We both knew this wasn't long term, and we were having so much fun with it that the end snuck up on us." She smiled softly and held out her arms. I went willingly. "If all we have left is a month, then we'll make do," I said.

Freddie wrapped me in her arms and kissed the top of my head as I wrapped my arms around her waist. "I think that's a brilliant plan. You asked me about my list. Maybe we can see how many we can check off before I leave."

"Now you're talking." I snuggled my face into her breasts, and she laughed. When I picked her up off the counter, she gasped, which pleased me. "But tonight, I'd like to introduce another method of mutual gratification."

"Oh?" she said with a squeal as I walked her back to my bedroom. "What's that?"

"Simultaneous oral."

"Oh!!" she laughed as I dropped her onto the bed and crawled up her body.

We removed clothes as I gave instructions. As always, Freddie was a fast learner.

THE TOY SHOP

FRANCESCA

After a night of mutual gratification, leading into a day of working with the resort patrons, I felt a little tired, though equally energetic. It was an added benefit of dating Eilidh that I hadn't expected.

I wasn't sure if it was the euphoric afterglow of sex or some kind of energy transference as part of her demi-goddess nature. If I were to ask my parents, Gavin would say I needed more evidence to rule out one or the other, while Brice would tell me to live in the moment.

Eilidh wanted me to stop by the club on her dinner break tonight. We hadn't tried another dinner during her working hours, though I'd make dinner and drop it off at her office sometimes.

Cooking for her was another experience I enjoyed. I especially liked it when she came to my apartment after work and showed me how grateful she was for the meal. I wondered if Da wooed Daddy with his cooking. All this time, and I'd never asked either of them. All the stories I read and the languages I knew, and I never asked my own parents how they had met. Their love seemed so complete that thinking of them as two separate individuals seemed strange to me.

Javier smiled and led me back to Eilidh's office when I arrived at the club. She was already there, working on something at her desk. When she looked up, her smile invited me in. She wore an off-white sheer princess-cut dress that hit her at the knees with some kind of styled, dark-colored bra under it that framed her breasts but left her nipples uncovered. Her panties were the same color and lace to match the bra. I wouldn't have known that she wore less sheer clothing if we weren't sleeping together.

She stood up from her desk and walked over to me. "How was work today?" Eilidh asked as she kissed me.

"Good. No last-minute proposals or large parties. It's been a quiet day." I touched her arm just to feel the dress's fabric and her skin under my hand while I tried not to take a deep breath. I knew I wouldn't want to leave Eilidh's office if I did.

Eilidh took my hand and led me back out of her office and down a side hallway until we popped into a shop from the back entrance. While I knew the resort had all kinds of shops, it never crossed my mind that one of them might be a sex shop.

The shop was warm and had dark tones that conveyed intimacy and mischief. The shelves had helpful signs above them that stated what toys, devices, or products were meant to do. I stared for a long time.

"How overwhelmed are you right now?" asked Eilidh.

"Somewhat." I liked that she asked me. This was certainly unfamiliar territory. Another experience to check off the list. I swallowed as I tried to steady my nerves. "I've read about vibrators and such, but I guess it didn't occur to me just how much or how many different things could be involved."

Eilidh grinned. "We'll start slow. Okay? The two main things we'll focus on for this trip are items that involve penetrative sex." She kept hold of my hand and led me over to a very impressive wall of phallic items.

"These are all the various shapes, sizes, and styles available. You can see that some are more natural than others."

I noticed one called "The Dragon," and laughed. "That's not what a dragon's penis looks like." First off, it was way too small in size, and second, they didn't have the protrusions the one on the wall displayed. "It would be more accurate, based on anatomy, to call it lizard-like."

"Noted. Maybe sometime you could show me the real thing."

Did Eilidh ask me to have sex with her, not in my bipedal form, but as me? I froze for a long moment. She surprised me, and I liked it, but I didn't know what to say to her suggestion.

"We can table that for now." She took my hand and spoke softly. "What I want you to focus on is what you might enjoy or would like to experience."

The variety ran all the ranges. Fae, ogre, dragon-lizard, something, tentacles, and shifters. There were even ones shaped like different historical figures. I had no idea why someone would want to be penetrated by a historical figure, so I ignored that part of the wall for the time being. The human-looking ones seemed less interesting by comparison. Even the multicolored, slightly curved, nondescript ones looked more attractive. But if I were to start somewhere, I figured it would be with something close to human without being over the top.

"This one seems appropriate." I pointed to one that had a similar skin tone to mine.

"That's a good choice. It's human-like, approximately seven inches long and 1.5 inches in diameter, and isn't too heavy for a harness," said Eilidh as she plucked the object off the wall.

"Why did you take it off the wall?"

"So I can purchase it."

"Why?"

"So we can use it later."

"Oh. Oh! Is that why you asked me here?"

She leaned on me a little. "Of course. You wanted to experience a certain kind of penetrative sex." She pointed out. "And I thought this might make your initial experience more gratifying."

"Is penetrative sex that bad?"

Eilidh shook her head. "No one starts out as an expert, but everyone can learn something about themselves through their partners." She leaned in. "Wouldn't you enjoy learning how to use yours?"

I felt my face heat, but I also understood. I liked this idea a lot. "Alright. What else do we need?"

By the time we were done, we'd purchased several different dildos, a harness, a vibrator, two sizes of anal plugs, and lots of lube. One even had a mint flavoring. I wasn't sure if we would ever use it all, but part of me was very interested in finding out.

Later that night, Eilidh came over. She was still dressed in her work clothes. I'd changed into a T-shirt and shorts and hadn't thought about dressing up. It seemed unnecessary to me. But I could appreciate that Eilidh was comfortable in her revealing outfits.

"Are you planning on admiring the view the rest of the night, or do you want to ask me in?" she said with a smirk.

Oh! "Please, come in." I watched as she walked in, her ass swaying, and her calves flexing in the laced-up sandals she wore. She put our purchases on the coffee table in my living room.

When she straightened up, I walked behind her, pecked her on the cheek, and wrapped my arms around her waist. "Do you know how incredibly hard it was to hug you instead of touching your ass?"

Her laugh sent pleasant shivers along my spine. "That's the point of the outfit. To make people look, and want to touch, or even ask to touch and be denied the pleasure."

"Is that what we are doing tonight?"

"No." She patted my arm. "There are a lot of reasons people enjoy that kind of tease or kink. It would be very irresponsible of me to make you endure that."

"Why?"

"Because you're enjoying being sexual and understanding what works for you." She turned in my arms to look at me. "If we venture into different kinks now, it wouldn't let you decide what you like first. It needs to be your decision. Exactly like how you picked everything out today. We don't have to use any of it. However, it was important that all the selections were yours. Choice and consent are important, especially where sex is concerned."

"You're still in work mode." It sounded like a counseling session I overheard her give a potential client once. I appreciated it wasn't for show. The candor we had with each other was important to me.

"I apologize, but only a little. If you decided tomorrow that none of this was for you and you'd rather spend our time together cuddling and watching movies, I would respect your choice. And I would hope that anyone you were with would do the same."

I held her and then slowly leaned in for a kiss. I liked our kisses the most, and I knew it would be the thing I missed the most after our time together ended. "How about your choice? Is this what you would like to do this evening? Play with sex toys?"

She grinned. "I'm game if you are."

"Hmmm, I have a specific thing in mind. Something I've been thinking about all day."

"Oh?"

Thirty minutes later, after she helped me with the harness, I had her bent over the end of my bed with her dress around her waist, and her panties slipped to the side. The initial insert was tricky, but once I managed it, I felt the urge to move my hips.

"Does this feel alright?" It felt okay, but it also disconnected me from what Eilidh felt. Even more frustrating was the urge I had to shift and use myself rather than a proxy. I hadn't focused on shifting parts of myself before. I'd been an all-or-nothing dragon, though some of my older cousins could, and when I asked, they shrugged. Either you could, or you couldn't.

"It's a nice pace." She sounded supportive, but not really into it yet. "You can take your time with it, but if you want to stop, just pull out." She was panting slightly, but it wasn't anywhere near the reactions I've elicited from her before.

I stopped. Eilidh rolled to her side, facing me as I sat on the bed. I removed the harness and set it aside. "Is it odd to say that I liked it but didn't at the same time?"

She shook her head. "No, that's a reasonable response. Sometimes our imaginations don't live up to reality. What works for some doesn't work for others." She reached out her hand, and I took it. I lay on my side and faced her as our legs dangled off the bed. "Would you like to try something else?"

My frustrations were odd. It wasn't that I didn't like it. It was more like I didn't like that it wasn't part of me. I felt like I was chasing a sensation just below the surface. "Do you trust me?"

"Of course, Freddie."

"I have the weekend off. Could we spend it at your place?"

Eilidh smiled. "Sure. I'll make sure we have all our favorites on hand. Is there anything else you would like?"

I shook my head. "You and a fridge full of food are perfect."

She laughed, and I kissed her, then rolled her onto her back and pressed myself into her at just the right spot. We adjusted a little as she put one leg on my shoulder. Now this made more sense. The contact and rhythm of our clits touching and grinding into each other.

Her panties were in the way, so there was a frantic pause as she stripped down more, and we moved further up on the bed. I rolled my hips as I sucked at one nipple and then the other, still trapped in the webbing of her bra. Her moans increased with each movement of my hips and every suck and lick I applied.

Eilidh's hand pressed into my breast and pinched lightly. I bit my lip to keep from crying out as the warmth built between my legs. Even though Eilidh had protection, I was aware enough to ask.

"Do you want me to come on you?"

Watching her process what I said was slightly amusing. I saw the realization click in her eyes, and she nodded. "It's okay. We were tested. We're safe. It's safe." Right. Precautions. Trust. Safety. Understanding.

I leaned down to kiss her, and our tongues met with each pass of our lips. Each thrust and grind made us more desperate for release. When I squeezed her breast, it was enough to drop her into that sweet endorphin rush. She shivered under me, and I kept going. The bliss was right there for the taking. Things tightened in my body, and it occurred to me that this was the first time I was aware of what was about to happen. Before, I'd dropped into it with no idea of how close I was. Tonight, I knew I could chase it or hold off. The profoundness of the moment sent me into my orgasm as I bucked into Eilidh.

"Fuck, Lee. Oh, fuck." I kissed her as my mind emptied and my body spasmed. Our fluids mixed, and I kept pushing into her, if only to make it last. She caressed my shoulder, which was her gentle sign of giving up for the moment. I dropped my head to her breasts and breathed heavily while she ran her hands along my back.

"That didn't take nearly as long as the last time we tried that," she said. I could hear the smile on her face.

"I was motivated."

"I'd say," she said with a soft giggle.

We curled up with each other, and I was content but determined. I wanted to be with Eilidh as my dragon self. I needed to see what was possible, and I wanted to try with her.

A DEN OF DELIGHTS

EILIDH

There was a knock on my door at eight o'clock in the morning. I lifted the eye mask off my face, a bit surprised to have someone outside my door at such an early hour. One robe and slippers later, I approached the door with trepidation.

"May I help you?"

"Lee, it's me."

I fumbled with the handle to open the door. Our conversation about the weekend had been brief. I hadn't thought she meant to start so early.

"Freddie?" She held a knapsack, two grocery bags, and a bouquet. "My word, come in." She made a beeline for the kitchen as soon as she crossed my threshold. I closed the door and leaned my head against it. "Did we plan to meet this early?" She wore a plain T-shirt and shorts, and her hair was tightly braided against her head. I'd never seen her wear her hair like that, but it was no less beautiful than her natural style.

"No," she said in a cheery voice. "I wanted to surprise you with breakfast." My kitchen was undoubtedly larger than the one in her apartment. So when I rounded the corner and found the bouquet in a vase and a steaming latte in my favorite mug, I was instantly charmed.

I took my beverage to the island counter and sat down to watch her work. "What did you have planned this morning?"

"How does French toast sound?"

"Divine." I was about to take a sip when I noticed she wasn't prepping; she had already prepared. There was a small bowl of fresh whipped cream, another bowl with her egg mixture, and another that looked like cinnamon and sugar. Then she pulled out an omelet pan and cut off a chunk of butter from a stick she withdrew from her bag. Then she pulled out a container of challah bread that smelled freshly baked. "How early did you wake up this morning?"

"I didn't." She brought the burner up to temp, and it melted the butter quickly as I watched.

"You didn't sleep?" I looked at her with a bit of surprise. I hadn't known her not to sleep before. Even when we stayed with each other, she slept peacefully.

"I wanted everything to be perfect. I have an entire menu planned for the weekend."

"Menu?"

"All your favorites."

"Really?" I knew I talked about food, but I hadn't expected her to cook the entire weekend. I thought we'd spend time doing other things. "What about watching movies and having sex?"

The question caught her off guard for a moment, and she nearly dropped the slice she had just dipped in her egg mixture. "Well, yes, that too. But I wanted to make sure everything was perfect this weekend."

Perfect because it was the last weekend we'd spend together before she went home. I couldn't help but smile. I set down my mug and walked back into the kitchen to wrap my arms around Freddie's waist and kissed her on the cheek. "It'll be perfect because we're together." Call me silly, but I meant what I said.

She turned to give me a proper kiss in response. "I want us to remember this fondly. I've read that sounds often triggered memories, smells, foods, and even sensory input. We will pack the weekend with all of it so we can remember it."

"Well, however it turns out, I know it will be memorable already." She smiled at me as she plated the first few slices of French toast. I went back to my seat and my morning latte.

A sprinkle of powdered sugar, a dollop of whipped cream, and a few slices of strawberries with a light drizzle of maple syrup, and I was somewhere between orgasmic and ravenous after the first bite. "This. . ." I pointed at the plate with my fork. "It's perfection, Freddie."

"I know." She grinned as she watched me take another bite.

"Are you going to join me?" She nodded as she quickly made her own plate and sat next to me. At some point, grapefruit juice appeared, and I hadn't even noticed. I didn't even realize she knew I liked grapefruit juice. It was the perfect tartness to counterbalance the sweetness of the breakfast.

We ate in companionable silence, then when we were both finished, she spirited away the plates and kissed me as she hustled past. "I'll take care of this while you do your morning things."

At this rate, dating anyone else might be hard. Freddie was setting the bar relatively high, and while it was indulgent, it also worried me. Would all this make it harder to say goodbye? I tried not to think about it as I left the kitchen to her and prepared for the day.

Thirty minutes later, I emerged from my bedroom wearing jean shorts and a tank top. The tantalizing smells of lavender and bergamot were in the air. They were two of my favorites, and perfectly balanced so that one complemented the other. I realized the smells were coming from candles when I entered the living area. "Alright, I'm intrigued. Are we watching a movie or having a spa day?"

I hadn't thought about going anywhere, but Freddie stood at the sliding glass door to my patio and held out her hand. "I'd like to show you something of mine."

"Okay, sure." I slipped my hand into hers, and she turned and walked through the sliding glass door—without opening it. "Freddie!" She held onto my hand as we crossed a threshold and landed somewhere else.

The center of what looked like a cave was a raised stone platform. On the platform was a long pad, similar to one you'd see on a massage table. Lit candles, with the same scents from my living room, were placed in different nooks in the surrounding walls. Next to the platform was a stand with a bottle of oil. So far, I liked where this was going.

"Where are we exactly?"

"My den. I set it up in the doorway to your garden." She led me to the platform and had me sit on the end.

"Your den, as in your dragon den?" She nodded. "Oh, my. I'm honored, Freddie."

She smiled. "I wanted to share this space with you. You're important to me, and I wanted to give you something of myself to remember me by."

I touched her face and tried to keep the tears from my eyes. "Freddie." I took a deep breath so I wouldn't ruin the gesture. "Thank you. It's amazing."

The smile on her face widened into a grin. "Oh, it will be." She reached for my tank top. "May I?"

We quickly stripped off the two articles of clothing I wore. Freddie helped position me on the platform, then rolled me onto my stomach. I half-wondered what would be next. I didn't quite expect her to put oil on her hands and gently massage my temples. By the time she reached anywhere erogenous, I was half a jellyfish.

"Tell me to stop if you become uncomfortable," Freddie said.

"Uncomfortable?" I think I said, but I wasn't sure as I was half dozing from receiving all her attention. Then she gave me a gentle swipe along the crack of my ass, waking me up a little. With each pass between my thighs, she spread my legs, and I went willingly as her fingers continued to explore into more sensitive territory. The oil tingled as it slipped along my ass and pussy. I had become sensitive enough to moan with each gentle brush of her fingers. When she finally pressed her slick digits into me, I pressed back onto them. Her fingers quickly worked me into an orgasm as they made sloppy wet sounds that echoed in her den. My lusty moans resonated as well, happy for the few moments the pleasurable wave lingered.

As I pondered what I would do to reciprocate, Freddie coaxed me onto my knees and slid between my legs, her mouth touching down and tongue flicking out to brush against my asshole. She lavished my ass with attention until I came, then drifted further down, tracing my labia with her tongue until her lips reached my clit. After I had three or four—because who really counted at that point—hard orgasms, I called for a break. When I turned over to look at Freddie, I noticed she had stayed clothed the entire time.

"Well, this won't do. How am I to reciprocate when you're not naked yet?"

She smiled and bent to press her wet mouth to my lips. We teased each other with gentle touches as our lips parted and her lovely tongue played with mine. I assumed her excitement, and the ardent kisses, came from whatever she had planned next. "I wanted to make sure I satisfied you first," she said quietly. "Because I want to show you who I really am, and it might make reciprocating complicated."

I kissed her again and touched her shoulder. "I promise, whatever you have, I can work with it. You won't leave this place unsatisfied."

Freddie blinked. I don't think she expected me to be prepared for what she was about to do. Since I'd known she was a dragon, I had hoped she'd be brave enough to let me be with her while she was in her natural form. I remembered her tongue on my face the first day we met. My imagination had only grown from there.

She watched me as I watched her strip bare, then shift. She was taller than my bungalow. Her scales were mostly black, with red along her back, belly, and wings. There was enough light to make out hints of green and purple undertones. The only noise was from the platform as it lowered, and she moved closer. When the platform stopped, I felt her warm breath as she straddled it and me. The sight of her was magnificent.

A soft limb touched my leg, and I looked down the length of Freddie's belly. When I realized it was her penis, I giggled. "You're right. It looks nothing like the one in the shop." I heard a chuffing noise and realized she was laughing. "May I touch you?" An affirmative noise followed, and I reached for her very erect phallus. The closest I might compare it to is a horse, but it was much larger than any I'd ever seen. The sensation of the cilia along my palm felt like a combination of very short fur or crushed velvet because they were so close together.

The moans Freddie made as I touched her were endearing, and it encouraged me to try more. I lay back and brought her penis to rest between my breasts. It was too large to do a decent job of it, but when Freddie caught on to what I was doing, her hips moved ever so slightly. She dropped a little lower, and I added my thighs to either side of her cock.

I heard nails scrape against rock as she held onto the platform and made small thrusting movements. I added touches from my tongue, just enough to tease, and she moved more. The small grunts and moans were lovely, and the oil I had on me worked like a charm. Her cock pulsed and heated against my skin. A moment later, I was covered entirely in dragon spunk.

There was a ticklish sensation as she licked her ejaculate from my body. "That was amazing, Freddie. Did you like it too?" She made another affirmative noise, or I took it as such. Another lick made me giggle, then I felt another sensation besides her tongue. A pulse of magic went through me like a mild electrical shock. The feeling of it was powerful and erotic, as the new-found source of magic enhanced my own. "Oh, my goddess! Freddie! Did you know your load was magical?"

A noise that sounded like a question made me realize she might not know. "Let me show you." I reached up and touched her snout. I could do things as a demi-goddess, but I didn't because it took a lot of power. One such ability was to make a mental connection. "Can you understand me?"

"Lee? You're in my head!"

"I am. Because you gave me magic! I feel like I could conjure a forest with this much magical energy."

"Oh? How fascinating. The lust smell is stronger too. It didn't go away this time."

"Does it bother you?"

"No." She paused. "It makes me want to do more with you. Especially now."

I bit my lip. More. I wanted more, too. This much raw magic gave me ideas. "Freddie, back up a moment. Let me try something."

As Freddie backed away from the platform, I created an incantation that changed my size. Gods and goddesses of old were larger than life. Literally, they could be mountains or people. I only needed something in between. I stopped the spell when I reached a similar size proportion as Freddie.

We looked each other in the eye for the first time since she had shifted. The dragon was clearly surprised. "Could you remove the platform? It's digging into my hip."

Freddie reached out a clawed hand, swiped the air, and the platform disappeared along with everything around it.

"Now, where were we?"

Freddie licked my neck and breasts as she slowly moved into place. I spread my legs and let her find her way. Dragons had slightly tapered penises, so when she initially pushed into me, it wasn't overwhelming. As she pressed further in, I grabbed her forearms to slow her down. She gave me a moment to adjust. Her eagerness showed she had never done this before. I touched her snout, and she made a contented rumbling noise. She sounded elated when she communicated via our link.

"Lee, you feel so wonderful. This is wonderful. It makes me feel euphoric." She rubbed her jaw and cheeks along my breasts while her tongue flicked along my sensitive nipples.

"Do you want to fuck me, Freddie?" With an affirmative response, she pulled herself out slightly and pushed back in. "That's my wonderful dragon. Let yourself go. You know I'm not fragile."

She took me at my word as she made quick thrusts into me. The effect was akin to being stuffed overly full, as the head of her pressed into my cervix, then somewhat stayed there while the rest compressed and contracted as she moved. Each undulation hit every erogenous part of me. The thickest part of her bumped into my clit with every thrust.

It wasn't long before I came, drenching the floor, which only encouraged Freddie to keep going. Her scales rasped softly against my skin, causing an interesting sensation. Without the oil on my body, her scales would have caused a great deal of friction. The experience was all at once erotic and enlightening.

Freddie's breathing changed, and I remembered it from the first time she came. "Are you almost there, sweetie?"

"Yes. But I want to make you come again."

That wouldn't be a problem. I adjusted my hips slightly and lifted my ass to meet Freddie's thrusts, and it did us both in. We were a mess of massage oil and fluids. Freddie moved slowly and deliberately watched where she put her feet. The euphoria and bliss were still there, but minor pains made themselves known.

Even with the aches and pains, I thought about other positions we might accomplish. Freddie ran her tongue along my body, then delved between my legs and licked at sensitive parts. It turned into a fantastic tongue fucking as she held my legs open with her forearms and clawed phalanges. Dragon tongues were longer than I suspected, since I never once felt a hint of teeth on my stomach or ass, though I saw her upper jaw hover above me. I'd have to ask later if dragons could dislocate their jaws like snakes could.

"Fuck yes, Freddie, that feels wonderful." She fucked me with her tongue, and I didn't know how to do anything other than respond. When she finished with me this time, I felt pinpricks along my thighs where her claws punctured my skin ever so slightly.

As I lay there and caught my breath, she materialized up a mass of bedding and pillows under us. "A nest?"

"Only the best for my Lee," she thought to me. I remained the same size as we curled up together. Her dragon head was on my thigh, careful of the spikes, and my head rested on her hip. Her warmth kept me from shivering as we slept.

When Freddie had suggested we'd spend the weekend together, my imagination hadn't even broached the reality we'd created. Our sexual desires were only limited by bodily functions. We explored so many configurations; I lost track, and we joked about making a picture book to remember them. Freddie seemed to have unlimited energy. Not only did we fuck nearly every chance we could, she insisted on feeding us tasty dishes from the menu she planned. She even replicated her father's smoked lamb and leeks to near perfection. By Monday morning, my fridge was empty. Both of us were beyond blissed-out, bruised, and marked from the experience.

We both spent the morning preparing for the day ahead, sharing the one piece of grapefruit that was left and a cup of coffee she'd made. There was a feeling of contentment mixed with a bit of sadness, as neither of us wanted to break the magical time we'd shared, and yet we knew our time had run out.

She and I went to the café that morning. I usually didn't because she had to be up early, but today she was scheduled for a late morning shift. I planned on doing accounting work in my office to catch up before client meetings later in the afternoon.

"Will you come by tonight?" I asked.

She nodded. "Most of my room is packed. I'd rather spend my last week with you, if you don't mind too much."

"Not at all." I gave her a soft kiss, squeezed her hand, and let her go. "Have a good day."

"You too!" she called over her shoulder as she went inside.

I took a deep breath and tried to move forward with my day. But every time I smelled or heard something that reminded me of the weekend, I smiled, and it created a brief pang of sadness in my heart. Whoever ended up being her mate was going to be extremely lucky. Freddie was a treasure, and I knew I would miss her more than any other lover I'd ever had in my life.

A Summer's End

Francesca

All my things were safely stored in my den, ready for travel, and I tucked my den key in my carry-on bag. I never told anyone that it turned out to be a book made of papyrus. Most keys were something common, like a rock or an item of some significance. The book was handed down in my family and initially kept in a case with other priceless tomes. But once I bonded with it, and it let me into my den space, it seemed indestructible. Which was good because it was really, really old, and I would have despaired if its knowledge were lost. I was still trying to learn Sanskrit so I could read it.

I loved parties. You could learn a lot about people at parties. When my parents discovered my precociousness after a gathering where I caused a stir by telling one group of adults what the other group of adults had said. When I was older, my Da invited me to dinner parties. He would cater, and I would listen to guests so he could have honest feedback about his dishes. It was fun to listen for clues or steer conversations into talking about the food, and no one the wiser that I was a ringer for the chef. Daddy loathed it, but I enjoyed gathering intel and mixing things up with large groups of people.

Tonight's party wasn't for social engineering, or at least not the kind I usually enjoyed. My coworkers and managers would all be there, and many of us were leaving for the season. While I was happy to go home, something felt wrong about it this time. Like I was leaving another home behind.

Of course, I forgot all that when Eilidh walked into the banquet hall. She wore a white and gold summer dress that flowed around her and accentuated all her curves. Her hair was intricately braided. She wore interesting pieces of glass jewelry that had gold flecks melted into the centerpieces.

We were circumspect as we drew closer to each other. I don't know if anyone ever asked Eilidh about our relationship. None of my coworkers asked me anything. That might have been because once I started dating Eilidh, I'd done little else besides work or read unless I was with her.

"You look amazing, Freddie. Is this Dior?" It was a strapless black cocktail dress with an A-line skirt and wide black tulle that acted as a secondary skirt with a bow around the waistline.

I shrugged a little and smiled. "One of my cousins works as a photographer at a fashion zine. Sometimes their jobs let them keep samples. When they clean out their closet, I've been lucky enough to snag a few things." It was the first occasion I've had to wear the dress since it was given to me. This was our last night together, and I wanted to leave Eilidh with a good impression.

"Well, you look amazing." I watched as she sipped her drink, and we stayed a good half meter apart. I didn't like that. For whatever reason, I didn't want to spend our last night pretending in public that we were only acquaintances. I set down my glass as a slow song started.

"May I have this dance?"

She blinked, then set down her glass as well. "Yes, of course."

I took her out onto the dance floor and brought her in close. "I missed you. Weren't we going to have dinner together before the party?"

"I had things to finish at the club." She tried to look me in the eyes, but failed. It didn't smell like a lie, but I could spot a half-truth from a kilometer away.

"Did I do something wrong?"

Eilidh shook her head. "No. But I have."

"Oh?" I wondered what she could mean by that. It's not as if we had made any promises to each other. If she'd been with someone else, I would have smelled it on her. Which I might or might not have understood. Something in me wanted to be upset about even the possibility, which made little sense. And her guilt and regret didn't make sense either.

"I know for you this arrangement wasn't based on an attachment. We never said we were in a relationship, but now that you are leaving, I find myself overwhelmed."

"Oh." We continued to move around the dance floor. "It's normal to miss someone you are fond of when they leave."

"That's just it, Freddie. I am more than just fond of you." She took my hand and led me off the dance floor. I followed until she stopped us in the corridor of the main hall that led to the shops in one direction and the hotel rooms in the other. "I tried to keep my feelings for you to myself. Especially since I'm not your mate, and after tonight, you'll be on your way home." She paused as tears slipped from her eyes. "I didn't want to ruin your last night here. Please forgive me."

I didn't know how to respond. Or what to say that would make things hurt less for Eilidh. I understood what she was trying to explain logically, but emotionally, I didn't have time to process what it meant to me. Before I could say anything, she squeezed my hand, then let go.

"Goodnight, Francesca." She walked past me and headed down the hall.

I didn't know what to do, so I said goodbye as well. "Goodnight, Eilidh."

The flight home was tedious. My favorite book couldn't soothe me. The seat was uncomfortable, and the food was, at best, palatable. I couldn't use magic to fix anything either because it was prohibited on flights. Three plane changes later, I was safely surrounded by Daddy's library, with a steaming mug of Da's tea and scones. It was familiar and, at the same time, cold. Even though a fire was merrily burning away, I had wrapped myself in blankets. I held onto my tea as if it was a lifeline to something, but what, I wasn't sure.

Gavin, my daddy, came into the library and fanned himself, the firelight reflecting off his dark brown skin, black hair cut close to his head in a fade, and golden eyes. Our bipedal forms shared similarities, where my dragon form looked more like Brice, my da. Da was the one that carried my egg. Daddy used to tell me stories about Da singing to me while I was in his stomach as he cooked in the kitchen.

"Freddie, it's too warm in here for the books. Why do you have the fire so high?" He came over to bank it, and the temperature dropped a few degrees. When he turned to face me, he looked concerned. "Are you alright, Freddie-bug? You're sweating."

When he reached to touch my forehead, I cried. I wasn't alright. Dragons didn't sweat. Something was wrong with me. "Daddy, I met someone."

All of my experiences with Eilidh came tumbling out of my mouth, even the sexual ones. I missed her, of course, but this was something more. There was a pain in my heart, and I wasn't sure what to do with it.

My parents called in our family physicians. The Alexanders were mage physicians who had treated our whole dragon family for years. When Leon arrived, he set to work. I hadn't met Leon before. He was one of the younger mages from the Alexander family, but he had the same dark brown hair and average good looks the whole family seemed to have. He asked if he could share with my parents when he found something, and I agreed. It was better to put their concerns at ease. I now knew what was wrong with me, but I didn't know what to do about it.

"Well, I can tell you it's not a mating bond. Her blood and pheromone markers haven't changed. However, I found a foreign substance."

Leon glanced at me, and I nodded, so he continued. "In the family medical documents, I found one example when one of your family members came into contact with an incubus and presented with the same foreign substance. The effects are akin to a drug, but it acts on pheromone receptors. Humans have died from withdrawal, but for dragons, it causes mild discomfort as the substance is flushed out."

Da frowned, mostly with his reddish eyebrows and crossed arms. "Didn't you say Eilidh was a demi-goddess?"

I sighed. "Eilidh's father was something else. I never clarified, and she didn't want to talk about it. At the time, it didn't seem to matter. I don't think she knew about this. She wouldn't hurt me." I couldn't believe Lee would have hurt me on purpose. Even in our last moments together, she tried to protect me in her own way.

Daddy knelt in front of me. "No, we know. You told us enough about your time together."

"It's possible the demi-goddess doesn't realize she has a latent incubus power. It heightens sexual pleasure, can induce euphoria, and has similar properties as dragon sperm. Having sex with an individual with this power would be highly addictive," Dr. Alexander said. "But, even so, with rest and proper treatment, we can deal with the effects of it easily enough. It only takes a little time."

Time. I had plenty of that now. My parents' library had seemed eternal to me, even timeless, before I left for the resort. Now all I thought about was how stagnant it was and lacking. Nothing made sense any longer. "How long will it take to wear off?" I asked.

"A few days at most. Your system is already breaking down the substance. I can leave a tea mixture you can drink to make sure it's flushed out completely." Leon offered an additional suggestion. "If you were to see the demi-goddess again, I'm certain I could reduce or eliminate the side effects of the incubus power with a charm or ward." My parents were happy with this treatment. I, however, found myself very upset about it. Even now, I couldn't quite remember how she smelled. Hints of it would come to my mind, and I would feel flushed with need and desire, only for it to disappear again. I had an irrational fear that once she was out of my system, I would never feel the same desire and lust I felt while I was with Eilidh. Even without her smell as a reminder, I felt a keen sense of loss. Our time together was short. How could I feel so much for one person in such a short amount of time?

After Dr. Alexander left, Daddy helped me to my room. He made sure the fire was roaring while I burrowed into bed with a mug of the doctor's tea at hand. "Would you like to talk about it?" asked Daddy.

"I don't understand." I honestly didn't.

"What are you concerned about, Freddie-bug?"

"She wasn't my mate, so how could I possibly have feelings for someone that isn't tied to me?"

"Oh, sweetheart." He kissed my forehead as fingers brushed through my hair, gently playing with the curls. "Sometimes we are fortunate to find that the individuals we're drawn to emotionally are also those we are biologically compatible with." He rubbed my back as I laid my head on his lap. "Take your Gram and Gramp, for example. They are biologically compatible, but it took them a long time before they had any genuine fondness for each other." He was quiet for a time, then sighed. "I never told you this, but I was in another relationship before I met your da."

This was news. "Who were they?"

"He was a very old mage. When I met him, we were doing research on the same subjects. We had an affair that lasted twenty years. He died in my arms and thanked me for loving him. He told me he was happy I wasn't his mate because he would have hated robbing the world of my beautiful face." Daddy's hand framed his own beautiful umber face as if it was a photo shoot for a fashion zine.

"He didn't." My daddy could embellish something fierce. It's why I loved his stories. But he only smelled of truth and love.

"He did! I promise!"

"Does Da know?"

Gavin nodded. "He catered the funeral reception. Mages have enormous families. Otto's reception was very lavish. His family spared no expense. A few bites of your da's food, and suddenly I had questions about the culinary origins. He answered most of them, and then a year later or so, I found out the same chef had opened a restaurant. I couldn't resist trying it, and Brice hadn't forgotten me, even a year later."

"Did he woo you with delicious food?"

"No, actually, it was boats. Turns out your da was great with boats before he took up cooking." Gavin smiled. "We spent a lot of nights together out on the water. Now that I think about it, it sounds really strange since he'd just started cooking. But the restaurant wasn't nearly as good or as popular as it is now."

The thought of my parents out on a boat a hundred or so years ago amused me. I didn't know why I had never asked before. I suppose books seemed more interesting to me until now.

"If I had known you were waiting in the library for your mate to walk through the front door, I might have said something sooner."

"I didn't know. As far as I was concerned, books were enough."

"And what about now?"

"I'm still in love with books." We laughed, and he patted my back.

"What about Eilidh?"

"There was something there, and it wasn't just her magic. It was more than that." I sat up so I could look Daddy in the eyes. "The last thing she said to me before I left was that she had feelings for me. I didn't know what she meant or how I felt. I thought it was because I was leaving. Now, I'm not sure."

"Why aren't you sure?"

"Because I think I have feelings for her, too."

Daddy pulled me into a hug and kissed my cheek. "Don't wait to find out, sweetie. Don't wait around for a mythical mate to show themselves. You deserve to be happy, okay?"

I nodded and wiped my face. "How have you two put up with me for so long?"

His face grew stern but was playful. "We did not put up with you, young dragon. We care about you, and we're your parents. So don't think for one second we would ever think there was anything wrong with you if you didn't have a mate within the first five minutes of walking out the front door."

"Everyone else seems to think that."

"Well, everyone else can take the piss." I laughed. Daddy grinned.

Once I stopped laughing, I realized where I should be. It was only a matter of planning. "Daddy, I have an idea."

RARE TEMPTATIONS

EILIDH

"Mr. Uluke said there's a new shop going in next to theirs. A bookseller of some kind," Javier said.

"That's nice." The numbers were their usual ebb and flow on the holo. Though some of the income had dropped off since I'd stopped participating in floor demonstrations and shows. Javier had tried a few times to cheer me up since Francesca left. Small gifts, surprise demonstrations from the staff, even an elaborate orgy night arranged for club members. After all that failed to lighten my mood, he took me for a long walk around the lake, which only made me cry more because the rocks reminded me of Freddie's den. This seemed to be his latest effort. He knew how much I loved to read, though even that seemed uninteresting these days.

"You should give it a try. Maybe you'll find something that interests you. Help you out of your funk."

"I like my funk, Javier. So let me be in my funk."

He came over and wrapped an arm around my shoulders. "If it were anyone else, I'd say take all the time you need. Unfortunately, mistress, your distress is catching. We know you miss her." He kissed my forehead, and I barely kept from crying for the second or third time that day.

It had been several weeks since Francesca left, and I still felt raw. There was no message or communication to say she was home safe. Of course, I didn't reach out either. I didn't want to presume. I had already assumed too much.

Her face said everything when I confessed my feelings. She hadn't reacted nor said anything. I'd been silly to think that there was maybe some small amount of something between us.

Javier was right. My mood was affecting everyone, and when your club was entirely based on the tone and mood you set, it did not make for good business. "Maybe I should take a vacation. I haven't done that in a while."

"You know we could manage without you for a short time, Ms. Eilidh. Your staff is well-trained. Maybe you could hire some guest tutors or instructors in your absence."

That was not a bad idea. "I'll consider it. For now, I think I'll leave this evening in your capable hands. Please call me if you require anything." I shut down the holo and gathered my things as Javier nodded.

I had intended to walk immediately to my bungalow. I had not planned on taking a detour into the shopping area, but my feet had carried me in that direction. Maybe it was the promise of the new bookseller that led me there. I wouldn't ever be sure. When I reached the shop, the sign above the door said "Rare Temptations," and when I looked inside, I held my breath.

Three people moved inside, arranging books and laughing with each other. One of them was Francesca. I didn't realize I was inside the store until Freddie looked at me.

"Damn," she said with such emphatic meaning my heart lurched and my eyes watered with unshed tears. But I held it in. She didn't want me here. Why else wouldn't she have said something?

I turned to go, and she called out. "Wait, please." I was outside the shop before she caught me by the arm and stopped me.

"I didn't mean to intrude. Javier mentioned a new shop, and before I realized it, I found myself wandering in this direction. I apologize." It all came out in a rush. Seeing her again was the last thing I expected. I hadn't even hoped she'd return for the next summer season.

"What for?" Freddie's eyes were wide, and she bit her lip. I wasn't sure what to do with that. "Lee, it was supposed to be a surprise." She smiled. "I wanted to speak with you first. I know

I made a mistake when I left. It took me time to see that, and I'm sorry I hurt you." She reached up and wiped the neglected tears from my face.

"I don't understand." I didn't, or rather, I wanted to, but also didn't want to hope for anything. It was too much after she left the first time.

"I was too literal." She sighed. "I didn't think my feelings were real since we were not mates. I didn't want to lead you on, if only to end up breaking both our hearts when I did find my mate."

"I suppose I understand that. But why come back?" Because that was the real question. Why be anywhere close to me if she was so determined to find her mate?

"Daddy told me about how he met Da. It was at a funeral for someone he cared about very much, if you can believe that."

It was undoubtedly odd circumstances, but it made me laugh a little, which was her goal, I think. Damn her eyes. I wanted to run, and I wanted to kiss her. It was all very confusing, and I'm not one to be confused about what I feel most of the time.

"He explained to me that no matter how long one lives, life is still fleeting. We can't wait around for the right moment or the right individual. Sometimes you have to be open to other possibilities."

"So, based on that, what have you concluded?" I was on an emotional knife's edge. I wanted to cry or scream. It hurt. Most of all, I didn't want to hurt any longer.

"I love you. I want to be with you for as long as you'll have me, for as long as we'll have each other. I could wait in a library and hope someone will show up, or share mornings with you and be your confidant. I want to sleep with you and next to you, and share my magic with you. I want a life with you, whatever that may be, for as long as it may be."

I wiped my face with the hand that she wasn't holding and burst into tears. "How in the world could I possibly say no to that?" She blinked as if the possibility of me uttering the word 'no' had not crossed her mind.

"I planned to make this more of a grand gesture, but maybe this is better." She tried to catch my gaze with hers, and eventually, I let her see my puffy face and red eyes. "I created a business plan with my parent's help. My whole family donated books to help me start. Some of them are even signed first editions. I wanted to show you the shop when it was ready. To see if you wanted to start again."

"What if I said no?"

She looked at her hands, then glanced back up at me. "I'd have to stay here for a year because I signed a lease. Then I would have spent that time persuading you we belonged together."

"Well," I inhaled and took a final swipe at my face. "I look forward to many days and nights of your persuasion."

Freddie frowned. "But I. . . I don't understand."

I smiled and shook my head. "Freddie, kiss me already."

"Oh! I see."

That kiss was our starting point. Everything that came before it, a prologue. Freddie's touch was akin to a home I had missed. Maybe her mate would show themselves in time. No matter when that was or what would happen, our time was right now, and I wouldn't let that go quietly.

When we finally came up for air, we held each other tightly, afraid to let go of the other for whatever reason.

"Would you like to meet my parents?" she whispered in my ear.

I nodded. "It would be an honor, my love."

Freddie grinned and led me into her bookstore.

Calm Heart

M.L. Eaden

CALM HEART

"Quinn," the ever-present voice hissed in my head, acting as an alarm waking me from my slumber. *"Is it today? Our treasure comes today, yes?"*

"You have a strange sense of what's important, Helmin."

The worm undulated across my body. Its mouth was burrowed into a spot on the back of my neck while its sinuous length was wrapped under my left arm and around my torso four times before it terminated via a connection in my navel.

Fae are born with unique abilities. Mine was the power of regeneration. Most diseases and physical harm will never affect me. It was the only reason the worm connected to my spinal column and nervous system didn't kill me, and the reason the worm developed sentience. We are forever connected, neither able to live without the other.

My constant companion, sharing our silent conversations. It is a wonder that my mental faculties have remained intact. But Helmin has rarely complained about our predicament until we started working with a client named Mateo.

"I do not, Quinn. Our treasure feeds me. I am barely able to maintain my higher functions from the wisps of life force you give me."

"That's ungrateful of you, considering we've existed for decades together, and you've thrived all this time, as the number of segments you have wrapped around my torso attests."

Throwing the bedclothes to the side, I sat up. Helmin slid along my abs the way a boa constrictor would tighten, then loosen again. Not quite agitated yet, but slowly reaching a point where I would need to feed us both.

I dressed in linen pants, a shirt with charms to hide Helmin's presence, and canvas sandals. At Firebaugh Resort, they knew me for my calming "energy." Those seeking to adjust their moods for the day often sought me out at mealtimes. In the employee dining area, I filled my plate with a variety of fresh foods and chose an empty table where my coworkers could join me.

The more anxiety, fear, or general worry they had in their life force, the more calming pheromone we created. They did not know what calmed them. I would breathe in the agitated and disrupted energy from their life force, which the worm processed, and we released a calming pheromone as a byproduct.

Originally, the worm's paralytic venom, once injected into a life form, usually killed it. With my ability, its venom had mutated my pheromones, creating a calming effect from the life force I would inhale. No one outside of my family knew of Helmin, and the fae stayed away from me regardless of how calm I seemed. My aura disturbed them, which wasn't surprising given the negative energies I often absorbed to feed my worm. Others have approached. However I never felt safe enough to engage a stranger, considering how they might respond to Helmin.

I had several coworkers around me, quietly eating. One was a luggage porter who was worried about their impending off spring. "I've never once seen you eat anything that looks remotely unhealthy, Quinn. Why is that?" they asked as they ate pancakes with enough syrup to make a small lake on their plate.

"I have never craved sugar. It was not something I grew up with. So it doesn't interest me as much." Their worry leaked out in the life force they radiated around them. I took large breaths, inhaling the invisible energy until their concern tapered off because of our pheromone influence.

Others came to the table, made small talk, and drifted away as they finished. Helmin was sated, but protested all the same.

"When our treasure arrives, we must enjoy them fully. I would leave your carcass for our treasure if it wouldn't kill us both."

Helmin was blunt, and its insistence that I do more than assist our steady client annoyed me. **"We've had this discussion. It's prohibited for staff to engage in intimacies with clients. So you will have to suffice with our usual limitations."** The familiar discussion was no less annoying now than it had been the first time we'd attended Mateo.

I had other clients with similar mental health issues who regularly visited Firebaugh Resort. My meditation classes eased most individuals' symptoms. They would leave feeling refreshed and well enough to continue with their own practice.

Besides the classes, I also assisted the spa with clients with a predator nature, or high prey drives. While the resort was a haven for many magical individuals, those same individuals were often apex predators. Most managed with only a passing influence from Helmin, so that they remained calm in the spa area. Others needed more attention. Especially as they were often territorial in their natural form. Of the many predators I've assisted, dragons were the most common, followed by vampires.

Mateo Valentino arrived at night, as his kind usually did. He would visit the resort once every few months to spend the week with me in private meditation. During those times, Helmin would gorge itself on Mateo's darker emotions and produce so much calming pheromone that I needed to be careful about where we practiced. While Mateo usually remained calm and in control on the surface, his emotions were often in turmoil.

Vampires have a muted life force until after they have fed. Mateo had often brought companions to keep himself in a higher state of bodily functioning. It was my only request when we began these sessions, as it helped him connect with his emotions and lessen his need to disassociate from them. It also allowed me to access his life force without taking too much from him during our sessions.

Our most recent encounter was different. I received a call from the front desk. Felven, our head concierge, melodic tones were less pleasant than usual. "I apologize for waking you, Quinn, but Mateo has checked in alone. He's asked to see you immediately. I tried to dissuade him, but he offered to pay whatever compensation you might require."

I blinked as I registered what Felven had said. Something was wrong. "Felven, how did he seem to you?"

Their translation device did little to cover the frustration that was clear in their sing-song tones. "Very agitated. Mateo said barely a word upon entering, then came to my desk and asked for you. He did not wait for a reply."

"Is he in his usual room?"

"Yes. I hope you are able to assist him, Quinn."

"I hope so as well. Thank you, Felven." I dismissed the call. Helmin made a delighted noise in my head.

"Our treasure is here! He needs us, Quinn. Hurry. Hurry."

"Yes, I understand, you glutton. But first, we will assess his situation. Agreed?" It did not answer my question and only became more insistent.

"Hurry, Quinn. Hurry!" I dressed even as the greedy worm repeated its litany.

We arrived at the corner suite, high in the resort's south tower. Usually, I would meet Mateo in one of the resort's many gardens. Only high concentrations of the calming pheromones affected Mateo. Because of the life force the vampire produced, we produced the pheromone in large quantities. While I have a higher tolerance for our pheromones, the concentration Mateo needed would dose me into unconsciousness in a closed space, hence the garden setting.

"Mateo, it's Quinn." I did not speak loudly, nor did I knock. Vampires had exceptional hearing. If he needed me, he would be nearby.

The door to Mateo's room opened, and I took a few steps inside. I did not sense Mateo or his life force. I took a few more steps into the room and was greeted by the spectacular view of the resort spread out in a seemingly peaceful desert by moonlight.

"Quinn." Mateo's voice was merely a rasp as the door shut behind me. The advantage of having Helmin was that it ate my own fears and anxiety, which made me an excellent individual to handle predators. It undulated under my shirt, which it rarely did. The movement threatened to disrupt the charms that kept it hidden.

One moment I stood alone, then the next Mateo stood beside me. He was shorter, decently built, with black hair and brown eyes. Those eyes told stories about his current state and his past.

He'd been a captive in the Necromantic War and made to do horrible things against his will. Mateo had belonged to a monastery then. As a scholar, he studied all manner of topics and writings. When Florentine's armies swept through, they raided the monastery. The entire coterie was swept into the war. Their collected knowledge was scattered or burned. It was nearly a year before he was captured by an allied necromancer. She broke his conditioning and warded his mind until they could move him away from the fighting. He convalesced for several months, remaining apart from others who had been rescued. During that time, Mateo discovered he was the only known survivor of his coterie. Since then, he had spent much of his time and resources regaining his coterie's knowledge.

The man who stood next to me in the dark hotel room was not the Mateo I knew. "Mateo, welcome." I hoped we were not too late to help him.

The predator relaxed slightly. He forced himself to take a breath and then another. It was our pheromones working, hopefully. Mateo would need to boost his life force to make the calming effect last longer than the anxiety and fear Helmin extracted from me.

He moaned his distress. "I am denied."

"Denied what, Mateo?"

"The covens I live near in New York. They wanted my coterie's collection, and my loyalty. I refused. They have denied me companionship."

"How?" This was curious. I had never heard of a vampire being denied those who wished to be companions.

"They marked me with a compulsion. My companions cannot come near me. I've subsisted on charity blood stores until I arrived here."

His phrasing struck me as odd. "Have you not fed?"

"My resolve is weakening, Quinn. My anger and rage threaten to consume me."

"There is a blood store—"

"No! I cannot stomach any more stale substitutes. With each sip, I'm driven more mad with need. My companions were the only ones that could quiet my thoughts." He sobbed, the sound filled with sorrow. "They cared for me, and I cared for them. The covens have no right to keep us from each other!" He grew more agitated as he spoke about his predicament.

I had initially thought it was to protect his food source, but it was more than that. I should have realized it. They had been an encouraging force for him. Protective to a fault, but they both seemed happy. Mateo thrived on their affection, certainly. He had told me once that he visited the resort and sought help at the pair's direction. Without the trauma from his past interfering, Mateo was a kind soul. I wondered, in this moment, how they dealt with him in this state.

"Mateo," he looked at me. I did not move. A tension filled the space between us. While I was not prey, I could not deny that his mental state affected me. "What would you have me do?"

"Help me."

"How?"

He took a step closer, leaned toward me, and placed a soft kiss on my lips. I was stunned. Helmin hissed with glee in my head.

"Take our treasure. Join with him. Share us with him. Please, Quinn."

"We need to be careful. He is not stable."

"We will make him so. Give him our blood, our life force. Let us feed."

In all the decades I'd been a host, I now understood the worm more. It saw a kinship, or a likeness to itself, in Mateo. Other than hunger, Helmin's other emotions were not always clear to me. Until now, I was unaware it could express infatuation. I thought its obsession with Mateo was because of its constant hunger and need to survive. It was now clear that Helmin desired Mateo for more than a meal.

Mateo tried to kiss me again, and I endured it for a moment before I gently pushed him away. "Circumstances as they are, I wish to help you first. Once your mind is clearer, we can talk." Mateo nodded in agreement instead of lashing out at the rebuff.

"Will my wrist be sufficient?" I'd never fed a vampire before, nor had I ever put myself in a situation where I needed to. I wouldn't have without Helmin's persistence. The anticipation I felt was not my own, but my body responded to it thanks to Helmin's connection to my nervous system. I rolled up my sleeve in preparation and tried to recall the room's layout to determine where this might be easily facilitated.

"I can smell your arousal." Mateo's hand ghosted over my body, but he did not touch me.

I sighed. "It's complicated."

"From my experience, arousal is the least complicated thing a body can do."

"I assure you, it is not as simple as it seems." I decided I'd had enough of the dark. "Living area, lights, five percent." The suite responded around us, raising the lighting to the requested amount. The dim light was enough to see by, and I slowly moved to the couch and sat. Mateo followed. "I am ready when you are."

He sat next to me, slowly blinked, then tilted his head. "Have I offended you?"

I shook my head slightly, "No." I swallowed, feeling Helmin's desire rush through my body. "Much the opposite. However, before anything else, I wish you to feed. Please." This was outside of the bounds of client privilege. If this did not quell him, I could not continue to allow Mateo to stay at the resort in his current state. The emergency warranted the action, so I told myself. Helmin said nothing.

Mateo gently took my left arm in his hands, bent his head over my wrist, and gave it a gentle kiss a moment before he pierced my skin with his fangs.

The pain was fleeting. As Mateo drew from me, Helmin vibrated, which caused me to convulse slightly. A groan escaped my lips as pleasure and lust flooded my system. It was not mine, but it became mine as Helmin swept me along in its desire.

"He feeds from us. Oh, joy. Oh, light. And then we feed from him. Our treasure."

"Our treasure," I whispered as my other hand caressed Mateo's head as he fed. He slowly stopped, licked the wound, and pulled away. The crotch of my pants was soaked with my semen.

Mateo blinked again, the blood filling him with life force. I watched as his agitation subsided. His gaze, along with a sly smile, was my first indication that he did not plan to let my verbal slip go nor ignore the condition of my attire.

"How long have you fancied me, exactly?"

I shook my head. "It's not me. Exactly. While I find you attractive, I work and live here. Intimacies with guests and clients are prohibited."

"Is that all that kept this revelation from me?" Mateo leaned forward slightly. "I would have met you anywhere you liked. I have enjoyed your company and often wondered if we would be compatible."

Compatible. Mateo was serious. It had been a very long time since I'd had a suitor. Because of Helmin, my life force and aura, and sometimes my calming pheromones kept any that might have an interest in me at an arm's length. I took a deep breath and blinked, realizing too late that there was too much calming pheromone in the room. "Living area, increase airflow, fifty percent."

My request was slurred. The system asked again, and I tried to respond. Mateo spoke up, and that's the last I remembered before I found myself laid out on the couch with Mateo patting my face, his brown eyes intently focused on me.

"I apologize for causing you to faint." Mateo backed away as I tried to sit up.

He reached out to help, and I instinctively took his hand, which gave me a jolt of life force heavily laced with anguish and pain. Helmin hissed and writhed as it gorged. I gasped and let go of Mateo's hand.

His soft laughter floated around my head. "I barely touched you, and yet you are aroused again. Though you say it's not attraction, I believe your body says otherwise, my friend."

My face heated with embarrassment, which was at least my own. My body shifted from a deep red to a shade of yellow to match. "I'll explain. Please understand. It means you no harm, and in fact, I believe it is rather fond of you."

"It?" Mateo said, clearly confused.

I slowly removed my shirt. The worm became visible as the charms in the shirt no longer touched my flesh. Helmin squirmed in delight along my torso, flexing and writhing with its desire for attention. If it had a face, it would have preened. "Mateo, this is Helmin."

Mateo stared at me for a long time. "Helmin. As in Helminth, the worm?" When his gaze returned to mine, he grinned. "The name also has Egyptian origins, meaning gentle."

I nodded. "When it began speaking with me, I gave it a name. I remember being delirious at the time. The irony is not lost on me."

"How long have you lived with Helmin?"

"A little over four decades."

"And you say it's the cause of your attraction?"

I nodded again. "Of all our clients, Helmin expresses itself more when we are near you. It even gave you a nickname." My skin remained a light yellow, marking my continued embarrassment. To describe Helmin's thoughts threatened to shade it darker.

"Some things make more sense now." Mateo sat back from us, and Helmin sent a shiver of worry through me. I held my breath. I did not know what would happen if Helmin were rejected. The worm's emotions never seemed that complicated before tonight. "The voice I heard during our sessions, it wasn't actually yours."

"Voice?" It was my turn to be confused. "What did the voice say?"

"That I was a treasure, and I could let go of my anger and frustration. To breathe deep and exhale, then relax." The fading yellow of my skin burst bright and seemed to glow in the room's darkness. "I had thought it was you and that you had some affection for me, but then I thought maybe I read too much into our sessions."

"No, well, at least one of us tried to maintain our professionalism."

"I am sorry, Quinn. I could not remain silent in the face of our treasure."

"Helmin regrets misleading you. We have lived with our secret for a long time. You are the first person outside of my family who knows of Helmin's existence."

Mateo nodded, eyes roaming my torso. He opened and closed his hands at his sides, controlling what I imagine was his desire to touch Helmin and me. It had to be his scholarly nature driving his curiosity. He remained calm even after he discovered our deception. "If you are comfortable discussing the topic, I would very much like to understand how you and Helmin became conjoined."

I gripped the shirt in my lap. With my arousal subsided, thankfully, so had most of my embarrassment. "I'll explain if you can give me a promise." It was no small thing to ask for a promise, especially for me. Most individuals knew not to make promises with the fae. They were binding in ways that were often unpredictable.

His face contorted for a moment; the weight of what I asked was evident in his eyes. "For allowing me to feed from you, I will grant you your request. What would you have me promise?"

"Promise that what I tell you about Helmin stays between us unless I say otherwise." Mateo nodded and repeated my words. After which I held up my arm. "Would you like more?"

He held my arm in his hands, then paused. "Will you faint again?"

"No, not from your feeding. It was because of our pheromones. We should be safe enough with the adjusted airflow."

Mateo held my arm and caressed it. "Safe? Maybe you should explain more before I drink again."

"Very well." I gathered my thoughts to explain. "As I understand it, the more life force laced with turbulent emotions I absorb, the more calming pheromones we produce," I explained. "Most of the time, we don't absorb enough to cause me or other living individuals around us any issue. What we absorbed from you while you were feeding was substantial, especially within an enclosed space."

"That's fascinating. I assume this was part of its original function, which then became modified after coming in contact with you."

"Correct." I nodded. "Fae often travel via a network we call pathways. They shorten distances and the time it takes to move from one place to another. Tunnel worms, much smaller than Helmin, can attack travelers. When this happens, the traveler is usually doomed. First, a tunnel worm bites, using its paralytic venom to calm its victim, who eventually slips into a coma with continued exposure. It then eats its way through a body, lays eggs, produces more, and continues the cycle.

"This one attacked me near an exit." I touched the back of my neck, remembering the sharp pinch I had felt. "My regenerative abilities kept it from calming me into a coma. However, it did not keep it from burrowing into my spine. Once it became attached, there was no way to remove it without killing me. Over time, I learned to live and even adapt to Helmin. This symbiosis has changed both of us. We discovered, after our initial bonding, I could draw on another's life force. Those with more turbulent thoughts or desires pleased Helmin most. My body modified the paralytic venom Helmin produces. Instead of paralyzing, it generates a calming pheromone which, while potent, is mostly harmless as it gentles those around me. It allows us to easily draw negativity from them, leaving an individual with a calm demeanor where previously they were not. These negative energies feed Helmin and allow us to survive."

Mateo smiled. "We are alike, Helmin and I. Feeding from others and providing our unique abilities in return."

"Oh, Quinn. Our treasure understands. He understands. I want to feel him, Quinn. His skin to ours. Please. Please, Quinn."

"How do you know that won't kill us? We collapsed from a single exchange." My attempts to talk some sense into Helmin were not working.

"Feed us. Feed us until we are full. Then we can touch. I want to touch our treasure."

I frowned. "I am at a loss as to how to explain what Helmin desires."

"Explain it plainly." Mateo grinned. I wondered if he had a sense of what the worm wanted. "No need to choose the right words."

"Helmin desires a pleasurable interaction. Which may or may not involve intercourse."

"I see. And how do you feel about it?"

I cleared my throat. "I am not opposed to the idea. However, if it feeds from your life force, the amount of pheromone we'll produce could cause us to remain unconscious for a considerable amount of time. It believes if we can attempt such an exchange and remain conscious, it can be sated, which could lead to more interactions."

Mateo frowned. "Do my wounds run so deep?" It was not the response I expected.

"Our abilities can only do so much. We are not unlike an adhesive plaster. We can lessen your suffering, buffer you from your emotions for a time, but we can not mend what's broken. To do that, you would need to take a different path."

Mateo was quiet for a moment. When he finally spoke, his words surprised me. "You both have given me more peace over the years than any other individual, including my companions. You and Helmin." He glanced over his shoulder at the view. "Come, I have an idea."

He did not reach for us as he stood. But he looked over his shoulder to make sure we followed. Once he reached the corner of the suite, he pressed a button, and the UV glass slid open to reveal a balcony. There was a cabana to one side and a hot tub in a dormant state. We followed him and watched as he pressed a button to raise the balcony's privacy curtains.

"I'll admit, it's a poor choice for our first encounter, but I'm more concerned with keeping you both conscious than having a better setting." He grinned. "At least until Helmin is fed."

"How do you know it can be sated?" Helmin seemed sure that there was an end to its hunger, but I'd never experienced it in all the time we've remained connected.

"As I pointed out, we are the same. There is sustaining one's self, and there is fullness. However, I will need more sustenance myself to help Helmin. Do you trust me?"

"It's not a matter of trust. I regenerate. It is my gift. You can not kill me no matter how much you take. Though I have never tested that theory."

"Have you already recovered from earlier?"

"Yes." I held up my arm. "Even your wound is gone."

Mateo came over to inspect my arm. "Most interesting. Though if I'd been more clear-headed, I would not have fed from you at all. You, being fae, could have had disastrous consequences. Many vampires have been destroyed from consuming mere drops of a fae's blood."

"Helmin makes us something more than fae. I believe that's why my blood does not pose an actual threat to you."

His hand slid along my skin, and Helmin shook across my abs. Our fingers laced together as he gently pulled me toward the cabana. While we stood there, Mateo stripped out of his shirt and pants as I watched. I realized rather suddenly that I had not been intimate with anyone for quite some time.

"Would you like me to help?" His question shook me out of my reprieve.

"No, I'll manage." I toed out of my shoes as Mateo crawled into the cabana. I watched as my brain processed the muscles and sinew that moved with a monstrous grace. Maybe it was not only Helmin that was interested. I removed my pants, folded them, and laid them atop my shoes before I went to the left side of the cabana. I moved to lie down next to Mateo and waited.

He reached out first and brushed my shoulder-length hair away from my face. The dual anticipation I felt sent shivers down my spine and changed the color of my skin to a light pink rose. Helmin was too quiet, likely focused on the sensations transmitted across our bodies.

A simple kiss, the second one of the night, tipped the balance. What was a mere touch of our lips blossomed into more, as I opened my mouth to his. The exchange of life force began immediately.

We tussled on the bedding and touched each other's faces. When Mateo touched where Helmin connected to my spine, I twitched as if he'd touched me internally. Helmin gurgled in my head. Mateo must have noticed something, because he caressed Helmin while he kissed me. I was so distracted I did not feel his fangs sink into my neck. I grabbed Mateo's head and held fast as he drank and Helmin ate.

Amid two like-minded beings, I became their vessel. I might have screamed in pleasure, except for our pheromones. Instead, I slipped from consciousness at the height of the pleasure we'd created, barely aware of the continued exchange.

When I woke, it was midday. I lay in bed with Mateo's arm over my side, his hand trapped between the first loop of Helmin's segments and my stomach. I carefully slipped his hand out and rolled Mateo onto his back. He was dead to the world and would be for at least another eight hours. I found myself envying his rest.

"Helmin?"

There was no answer from the worm. I'd never known it to remain dormant after I was awake. I left the bed and went to the bathroom to relieve myself. In the mirror, I saw the mess.

I had multiple bite marks and dried blood along my neck and shoulders. There was ejaculate across my stomach and Helmin's segments. I looked ravaged.

"Where is our treasure?"

The worm was awake. Good. "Sleeping. And he will be for some time." I didn't bother with keeping my words to myself any longer, not after last night.

"Mateo's touch was pleasurable. His agony filling. I wish for more intimacy."

"Well, you'll need to wait until he's awake. Right now, we need a shower and to eat."

"You were overwhelmed with pleasure. Mateo and I were surprised. You need more stamina."

I opened the shower door and sighed. "Shower on thirty-eight degrees Celsius, please." The water sprang to life, and I stepped into it. Substances ran from my body as I used body wash and a washcloth to clean myself.

"You're strong, Quinn. Why did your pleasure make you unconscious?"

"Maybe it's because I haven't been with another since before I became your host."

That seemed to quiet it. I finished cleaning up, then dried off and put on a robe since my clothes were likely still on the balcony. When I opened an audio call to the concierge desk, it did not surprise me when Felven answered.

"Good afternoon. May we assist you?"

"Hello, Felven."

"Quinn? Is everything alright?"

"Yes." I didn't elaborate, though Felven waited for an explanation. "Could you have room service bring me lunch and dinner? I'll be here until he wakes."

"Certainly. Would you like me to charge the room?"

"No, charge my employee account." Felven was quiet again. "And please cancel my appointments for today. I don't believe I'm scheduled to help in the spa, but I have a few classes this afternoon." And one I had already missed earlier. I had not missed a class in the decade that I had worked at the resort.

The quiet continued, and I wondered if I was disconnected. "Quinn, are you safe?" Felven asked.

That was a good question that might have been excellent to ask before now. "I'm safe. The guest is safe. No cause for alarm."

"I'll convey your sentiments to management."

"Thank you. I appreciate your discretion, Felven."

"Be well, my friend."

I disconnected the call and found myself with nothing to do but watch holo shows or read. I had access to many periodicals from across the planet and used the holo reader to open the New York Times, which covered most of the upper eastern seaboard. There wasn't anything unusual about most of the articles until I found one with the headline: "Valentino Household Missing After Estate Fire."

Covens were not to be trifled with. This was likely the safest place for Mateo. They would not dare to attempt anything directly. There were too many wards and safety measures. However, it would harm nothing to send a communication to Felven so that security would know if any members of the east coast covens arrived.

Lunch arrived via a hatch system set next to the door. Some companions had their own rooms. Others shared with their vampire host. The hatch allowed items to be passed through while maintaining the daylight security of the room.

That Helmin had not conveyed its hunger nor spoken was peaceful and slightly odd. As my constant companion, this was the first time I'd not experienced its hunger as a persistent need.

I spent much of the afternoon reading and meditating until early evening. When Mateo finally woke, I was eating my second meal of the day. He showered, exited the bathroom in a robe, selected a bottle of wine with two glasses, then joined me at the table.

"Do you drink?"

"No, not regularly."

"Would you like to join me?" I gave him a slight nod, and he poured me a third of the amount that he poured himself. "Did a slightly judgmental smile appear on your face just now?"

"It might have been a smile. I don't know if it was all that judgmental. More amused than anything."

Mateo smiled. "Amusement is acceptable." He took a drink. "Did you know your friend talks while you sleep?"

I nearly choked on my microgreens.

"By that reaction, I am guessing the answer is no." His smile spread to a grin. "Helmin was very affectionate with its words, albeit slurred. You're right that it's quite taken with me. Although I have to admit, I've never had a non-bipedal paramour."

"I was unaware that Helmin had that much control over my language and speech centers. I suppose I should consider myself lucky that it does not have a grasp of my gross motor functions."

Mateo slowly swirled the glass in his hand. "I wouldn't be surprised if Helmin develops that ability in time. The more integrated the two of you become, the more abilities it will work out for itself."

I couldn't decide if that bothered me or not, so I changed the subject to something more awkward, but one I knew I needed an answer to. "Did we have intercourse last night?"

"Strictly speaking, no." Mateo's smile dimmed. "It's not that I wouldn't have wanted to, but when Helmin spoke and said you were unconscious, we stopped what we were doing. Besides, it was near the time I usually sleep. So I brought you inside, and Helmin kept me company until the daylight took me. I do apologize for not cleaning you up, but Helmin thought it would upset you." Mateo set down his glass and folded his arms on the table.

My food seemed less appealing. "Thank you. Helmin was right. Seeing the evidence of what happened helped, though it did not occur to me to ask the worm what it remembered. I assumed it had passed out with me."

"How is Helmin?" Mateo picked up his glass again.

"Quiet, even now. It is the first time I have not felt its hunger." Mateo's smile returned. I found myself admiring his smile, his gentle face, and the ease of our conversation. While I pieced together the previous evening's events, Mateo was patient with me. "And how are you this evening?"

"Sated. Blissfully sated." Mateo reached his hand toward me, and I, who had not physically touched anyone in a long time until last night, found my hand gravitating toward his offered one. "You are a very remarkable individual, Quinn. Helmin is as well. I would like to make up for last night, if I may."

"Make up for it? How?" While we might not have had intercourse, I remember a certain amount of pleasure before

I slipped into unconsciousness. I wasn't sure I was ready for another night as intense as the previous one.

"Tonight is about your pleasure. What would you like? Helmin gave me its promise that it would assist." I must have had a shocked look on my face, because Mateo laughed. "Oh, come now, Helmin may be blunt, but it cares about you. Quite a lot, actually. Helmin was upset at first and thought we had harmed you last night. It was the one that stopped us when it realized what had happened to you."

That was a lot to process. I knew Helmin cared, but I thought it was regarding its survival and our connection, not actual concern.

"Maybe I should start with a few questions instead," Mateo said as he squeezed my hand, then let go of it. I missed the contact.

I shrugged. "You may, but I also reserve the right to not answer."

"Oh, playing a bit of hard-to-get, I like it." Mateo picked up his wine and finished it. He played with the glass a moment before he set it down. "I tend to woo people before I dine or have sex with them. I apologize again for the abruptness of everything yesterday. While you did consent, I felt it might have been under duress from the two other parties involved. So my first question is, did you enjoy last night, or did you feel left out or without a say?"

My mouth felt dry, so I picked up my wineglass and took a drink. "I felt—"so many things last night, but several words came to mind. "Included. Cherished." My gaze met Mateo's, and a smile tugged at my lips. "Accepted." After that, I felt brave enough to continue. "Last night was very pleasurable until I could no longer participate."

"Ah, we overwhelmed you."

"You did, though I admit I don't know what I should have expected. This is not something I've done before."

"Sex?"

I shook my head. "No, I've had sex, though I've not entertained the notion of having sex with anyone after I became host to Helmin."

"No one's approached you?"

"Many have, and I rebuffed their advances. It is hard to trust strangers with secrets you've kept because your family has taught you to keep them."

"Why were you honest with me then?"

It was a good question, so I spoke the truth as I saw it. "Helmin wanted more, and that was an influencing factor, but I realized after you accepted us, I also wanted more. That I should want more, with or without Helmin's interest."

"You seized an opportunity." Mateo smiled.

"Yes."

"Would you like another? Opportunity, that is."

"With you?"

Mateo nodded.

"Yes, I would very much so."

"Finish your dinner." He pointed at my half-eaten plate. "I'll make some arrangements." With that, Mateo got up from the table, poured another glass of wine, and took it with him to the holo interface. I finished my dinner, feeling I might need the energy for the evening ahead of me.

We agreed to meet an hour later in the lobby, which allowed me to return to my residence to change. It was then that Helmin spoke.

"You do not need to wear your charms. They itch. Wear better."

"You've never complained about my clothing choices before." The exchange from last night seemed to have a marked difference in Helmin. It made me wonder what else my Mateo did to change us.

"We were not with our treasure. I was not as aware. Dress better." How did it know what I was wearing besides the charms? Could it now see what I see? The thought was a little unnerving. I held my curiosity in check. There would be time enough to discuss with Helmin what else it could do.

I settled on black slacks, comfortable dress shoes, and a dark blue silk shirt. I braided the sides of my hair and twisted them together at the back of my head so it would stay out of my face and show off my pointed ears.

When it was time to meet Mateo, I used the employee passages to reach the front of the resort. The hallways were quiet this late in the evening. When I exited the employee door near the lobby, the only one present was Felven. They rarely slept, and from what I understood, they were very particular about their work schedule as well.

Felven's eyes widened, and their tentacles seemed to shiver slightly upon seeing me. "Greetings, Quinn. You look very appealing this evening."

"My thanks, friend." It reminded me of Felven's initial call when Mateo arrived. "Regarding my services for Mr. Valentino, there will be no fee."

"That's highly unusual. May I ask why?"

I smiled as Mateo arrived in the lobby. He was dressed for an evening out in slacks, a purple cotton button-down shirt, with a black tie that matched the evening jacket he wore, along with the dress shoes.

"No, Felven, not tonight." I left Felven's side as they made an interesting sound and joined Mateo as we walked out the front entrance to the waiting vehicle.

We entered the vehicle, and the automated driver pulled away, heading for whatever destination Mateo had arranged. We occupied the back seat together, and as the vehicle left the resort behind, Mateo reached for my hand. I enjoyed the feel of his hand in mine as Helmin practically purred in my head. When the vehicle arrived at its location, I smiled.

"A museum?"

"Well, yes, but that's not why we are here. This museum has a planetarium. I remembered one of our sessions where you pointed out the stars by their fae names. This planetarium does a presentation entirely based on fae stories."

"How did you arrange for it to be open this late?"

"Ah, well, Felven is a bit of a miracle worker."

It seems I wouldn't need to answer Felven's question after all. Once we left the vehicle, an attendant met us at the front of the building and escorted us to the planetarium. We selected our seats from the upper middle of the elevated area. As the show began, Mateo took my hand and held it while the holo presentation, along with a hologram of a fae dressed in a traditional garb of flowing silk robes filled with iridescent colors, presented our stories. Many of them I had not heard since I was a child.

When we returned to the resort, I escorted Mateo to his room. "Would you like to come in for a nightcap?"

"You're being very formal, considering everything from the night before."

"I am trying very hard to make up for the night before. I should have treated you with more respect and grace. My desperation made a mess of it."

"I don't think Helmin would agree."

"Helmin is still learning. Give it time," said Mateo with a smile.

The worm was still quiet. Except for my clothing choices, it had remained that way the entire evening. Maybe Mateo was right.

Mateo held out his hand, and once again, I took it. He led me into his room and then onto the couch. There I sat while he hung his dress jacket, then poured two single measures of fae spice whiskey. I had not seen or tasted it in a long time.

"Are you trying to make me drunk?" I took the glass from him as he sat next to me.

He shook his head. "I know the whiskey is potent, but mostly I wanted to make sure you felt welcome here. Not as my pseudo-therapist, not as hotel emergency management, but as my friend and someone I care about."

That was a marked difference. The entire night had been. To hear Mateo state why was something of a surprise. I took a sip of whiskey and was reminded of my youth. Bonfires and celebrations. Ceremonies and life. I looked at Mateo, and his life force was strong. His aura was peaceful. He was more stable than I'd ever seen him in all the years he'd visited me for help.

I drank a little more and set down the glass. "Maybe, before anything else happens, we should take a moment to observe."

"A reality check?" He chuckled, "Alright. What is it you observe?"

"While last night was somewhat of a necessity, and tonight has been pleasant enough so far, expectations of more seem like so much false hope."

"Why would you say that?" Mateo drank, and I took a deep breath.

"My life is here. You also have companions and others you are concerned about. Anything that happens here is temporary."

"I see." Mateo set down his glass. "You want to know my intentions."

I thought about that for a moment. "Yes. Please. I think that would be best."

He smiled. "I do not know what the future holds for me, but I do know that I would enjoy it less if you were not in it, in whatever way you wish. I would like to be your friend. Yours and Helmin's. I would like to be more, but that is for both of you to decide.

"My companions and others are safe. I know that much. But they are kept at a distance by the compulsion spell. If I could remove it, I would. But it would not make a difference in my feelings for you.

"As for tonight, my wish is to spend time with you. To show you, I can, in fact, behave civilly and maybe charm you a bit." He grinned. "I would not mind taking you to bed, either."

That made me smile. "I would not mind that myself. It has been a while." I noticed my skin color shift to a deep rose. Mateo leaned forward and kissed me. While some have called me reserved, I felt more myself than I'd been in a very long time. Each kiss made another crack in the dam that I used to wall away my emotions after my brush with death and transformation into Helmin's host.

Mateo unbuttoned my shirt as I undid his tie. He pressed kisses to my flesh and Helmin's as I worked at his shirt. Then a gentle nip from his fang at my ear made me gasp.

"Was that a good sound or a bad one?"

"Good. Very good."

"Excellent."

I sighed as I worked his shirt down his arms. He paused at his nibbling to do the same with mine. He nipped more, and I did not hold back the noises that my throat made in response.

"Shall we move this to a more comfortable location?" I made some noise in the affirmative. Mateo pulled away, which caused me to follow. We kissed and danced in circles until we found ourselves inside the bedroom. We discarded our shoes next, and then slacks, as we sought kiss after kiss. I fell back onto the bed, and Mateo followed. Each movement that brought us to the center of the bed pressed us closer together.

Mateo smiled as he kissed me a few more times and slid his hands along my torso and along Helmin, who was still quiet, much to my surprise. His hands slid further down and caressed the side of my ass cheek. As our tongues tasted and caressed lips and teeth, I moaned into his mouth. He moved on from my lips and worked his way down my torso.

When he licked Helmin's first ring of segments, the worm made some kind of squeak. Then, as Mateo reached my navel, Helmin squeaked more. I don't think I ever heard a sound quite like it, and I laughed.

"Am I tickling you?"

I chuckled and shook my head. "Not directly. Helmin is making odd squeaking noises every time you lick part of it. It's quite amusing."

Mateo grinned. "I enjoy making you laugh. You have a beautiful laugh." He gazed up at me with his brown, sultry eyes, and I took a deep breath while Helmin writhed around my midsection. "But let's see if I can continue to have you make odd noises, hmm?" Mateo shifted lower and kissed a patch of skin above my groin. "Your cock is magnificent. The redness of your skin makes it look like candy."

"Most fae appear like this when very aroused," I said, panting with anticipation.

"Ah, now what you said yesterday makes more sense. It really wasn't you, or you would have been this glorious color of red."

"Yes, exactly."

He took my cock in his hand. "Would you like me to see if we can make it a darker shade?"

"You're welcome to tryyyy, oh goddess." He put most of my length in his mouth and swallowed around me. I was not prepared. My breathing was erratic, and Mateo was too talented. I reached for his head and smoothed my hand over his silky black hair while gasping and bucking each time his mouth enveloped me. When I sank my fist into his hair, he took it as some kind of signal and pulled off, only to work me over with his hand. A bright blue substance left my body and splashed across my skin, which was so deeply red one might mistake it for black in a particular light.

Mateo had his face pressed to the inside of my thigh as my arousal subsided. "You are lovely. I could spend eternity gazing at your body and making love to you." He kissed his way along the body he proposed to worship, and I remained in my state of pleasure. His cock rubbed gently along my torso as he kissed and caressed his way toward my lips. Each time, Helmin made noises. It gave me an idea.

"Mateo, would you be willing to try something?" His nod and sly smile were encouraging. "Oh, and we'll need lube." His smile brightened even more.

At my direction, Helmin loosened around my body. I adjusted the segments so that there would be two groups of two. Testing the worm's creativity by giving it a challenge, I used the lube and my own spend to slick up Helmin's segments. Mateo understood.

He sat on my midsection as we carefully coordinated between Helmin's looped segments and Mateo's cock. The effect was startling.

"It's like nothing I've ever experienced before. Fuck, Helmin. Quinn, this feels wonderful." I wrapped my hands around his ass as he thrust between the segments. Two on top, two on the bottom as Helmin made any number of movements. I admired the view.

"Our Treasure is making love to me. To us, Quinn." Its happiness was nearly overwhelming, along with the satisfaction and pride it felt.

Mateo's powerful legs and ass flexed with each thrust. He was not a Grecian beauty, but his acceptance and understanding made him the most beautiful being in my eyes. I should have trusted the worm to have good taste.

"I'm close. Fuck, I'm close." He reached for my hands, and I held them to his back while his hips thrust forward. His whole body seized as he came across my chest and nearly broke my hands with his grip.

When I let go of him, he moved off of us, then collapsed next to me. I glanced out of the window and noticed how late it was. The morning was about to steal him away. "Helmin's right. You are a treasure."

Mateo's gaze met mine. "I can see it in your shining hazel eyes, the way they dance when you look at me." He sighed softly. "I'm your treasure." Mateo smiled, reached for my hand, and kissed my knuckles. "Helmin's and yours." He kissed me with his last moments, and then he was gone. Inert for the next twelve hours at least.

Helmin hung slack around my midsection, as inert as Mateo. "Are you alright, Helmin?"

"I am . . . content."

I smiled. "That makes two of us." My skin flushed with colors that matched the sunrise as I went about cleaning up Mateo and tucking him into bed. Before I retired for the day, I made another call.

"Quinn."

"Felven."

"Same order as yesterday?"

"Yes, please. And, could you—"

"I've already canceled your appointments for the week and put you on leave for the same amount of time."

"Felven," I said softly. They were indeed a friend. One I hadn't really known I had until now.

"If anyone deserves some measure of happiness, it is you, Quinn." Their melodic tones were a soft, joyous song. "You believe we do not see you, but many of us do, and we all hope for the best."

"That is my hope as well."

"Be well, my friend."

"The same to you, Felven."

I went to my rest as content as Helmin, next to a man I seemed to have a fondness for in such a short amount of time.

I woke up sometime later, relieved myself, and ate lunch. After I returned to Mateo and slept until my senses, or maybe Helmin, woke us. Mateo was fingering its segments as Helmin purred.

"I had no idea Helmin had such a range of noises. These past two days have been very enlightening for me."

Mateo laughed. "What noises is it making?"

"It's almost a purring sound, like a low hum, with a light thumping noise."

His grin was infectious. I grinned back as he continued his soft caresses. "I have to admit, I'm rather pleased that I have satisfied both of you to the point that you make noises or turn interesting shades of red."

And I was red. Deep red and hard. It was nearly painful. "Are you hungry?" Mateo's eyes shifted from their playfulness to something darker. I had offered myself again as a meal to a predator. Our predator. Our treasure.

"Will Helmin be able to feed?"

"Without driving us into unconsciousness? I believe so. Your aura is still fairly calm, but your life force is quiet and withdrawn. Your touch has cooled as well."

He leaned toward me and gave me a kiss. "We can't have that now, not for my paramours."

"Quinn, we don't mind. Tell him."

"Helmin begs me to point out that we do not mind your touch, warm or cold."

"Oh?" He slid his hand down further and wrapped it around my cock. It was cold, but not unpleasant to my heated skin.

We kissed as he used his hand to caress and tease. First fisting my cock, then cupping my balls. Before I could say anything, Mateo moved away. He chuckled at my gasp of disappointment, opened a drawer, took something out, and then returned to bed.

He held out the bottle of lube and a condom. "Fuck me, Quinn. Please."

I closed my eyes for a moment and sighed as I tried to control my excitement. "Yes."

Mateo lay on his stomach as I applied a generous amount of lube to his crease. When I explored with my fingers, it surprised me to discover a lack of resistance. When I mentioned it, Mateo chuckled.

"I'm mostly dead right now. So it will take my body time to respond to anything, which makes vampires excellent at receiving when we first wake."

I smacked his ass for the crass joke. He laughed more, and that delighted me. "Well then, I won't dally any further." My skin was beet red when I put on the condom, and I pressed myself into him. We both groaned as I sank into him completely.

"Fuck, you feel warm, hot even. Quinn. Please. More." I moved. Slow at first, so I would not spoil myself in a short amount of time. Each thrust was a near agonizing drag on my cock, creating a searing line between pleasure and pain. Mateo was content, it seemed, but I knew he would not truly be able to join me without blood.

His frame was light as I lifted him off the bed and pulled him back toward my chest. He moaned softly until I put my right forearm in front of his face. My left arm was wrapped around his middle while I continued to fuck him slowly. "Drink, Mateo. Fill yourself, our treasure."

The last must have aroused him because he cradled my arm between his hands and sunk his fangs in. Each pull made me feel my blood rush from my cock to my head and back. I grunted with the strength of it, but didn't stop pushing into him.

As he drank, his life force became more apparent. He woke up from the inside out. I knew he was finished feeding when he let go of my arm, and his lower half clenched around my shaft with such vice that I nearly came.

"Oh goddess, fuck!" I thrust into him faster.

"Yes, that's it. Fuck, you feel exquisite."

I held him tight as my arm leaked blood down his chest, and each thrust was a practice in edging myself until I could no longer stand it. When I finally came, it was with a roar and a half-sated vampire in my arms that wanted more.

Mateo moved away from me for a moment and retrieved his own condom. "My turn?" His voice was eager but patient. His cock was pressed to his belly, and my whole being, including Helmin, wanted what Mateo offered.

"Please, our treasure."

"As you wish, my loves."

I laid down, and Mateo didn't immediately start where I expected him to. He lay across my back and kissed softly. It built my anticipation for his bite, so I suspected, but it never came. Instead, he kissed my shoulders and then kissed Helmin at the point where it was attached to the back of my neck. I vibrated with need and desire again. So did Helmin.

He poured lube on my back and slicked up Helmin's segments. Then poured more onto my ass crease. While his fingers played with my hole, his other hand played across Helmin. The worm was so enthralled that it only made gurgling noises in my head. I was close to doing the same until Mateo coaxed me to my knees.

Mateo's initial push into my anus made me gasp. I was tight and needed to relax, but everything felt tense and warm. Helmin saved us as he produced calming pheromones from my mild anxiety. When I did relax, Mateo took his cue, wrapped his hand around three of the four ropes of segments, and used them as leverage to fuck us.

Even with all that tugging, Helmin never once complained. The euphoria the worm produced was very much at work and drove all of us toward our climaxes.

I came over and over again, in that space of bliss, but Mateo did not let up. I did not ask for mercy. Neither did Helmin. It was when Helmin and I were on the verge of passing out that

Mateo let go of Helmin, pressed me down to the bed, and sank his fangs into the back of my neck.

The noises I made were loud in my ears as we all came together. I could only hope the room soundproofing was still intact. Helmin gorged on any dark thought, which wasn't much, but enough to maintain our pleasantly calm high while we rested from our orgasms.

We lay together in a mess of blood and fluid, laughing softly at our own facial expressions. When I recognized the scar on Mateo's shoulder.

I brushed the mark with my fingers. Some of the pleasantness of the moment wore off. "It's the compulsion, isn't it?"

"Yes," Mateo said with a heavy sigh.

"Would you like me to break it?"

"You can break a vampire compulsion so powerful it can keep those tied to me by blood more than a thousand kilometers away?"

"Well, when you put it like that, I don't know," I said as I traced the scar. "Could I try?"

"If you are successful, I will do anything you like. You have but to name it."

I nodded and leaned over the scar. It looked like a crest. Likely one of the coven families that wished to make an example of Mateo. That angered me. How dare they mark him.

"Darling, are you alright?"

I noticed my skin color was a stormy blue, rapidly darkening like a sky about to split open and spill its heavy contents on the ground. "I am alright. I'm not upset with you."

"Alright."

"Lie still."

Mateo did as I asked. While I concentrated, I could see the thread of the spell in his aura. I grasped it in my mind's eye and yanked. Mateo gasped. I whispered a reversal as I held onto the tainted thread.

The thread sizzled and disintegrated as Mateo cried out. When I opened my eyes, the mark on him faded, and all that was left was soft, new flesh.

"They used a lot of power to maintain a vast distance, but not to secure the spell. It was easy to disrupt it." I was rather proud of myself.

"Very excellent work, Quinn. Our treasure is no longer marred, and he will have his companions again."

Ah, that was right. Mateo's missing companions. The reason he had needed us. I drew back from Mateo's enthusiastic kisses.

"I'm sorry. I didn't mean to overwhelm you." He was happy, and I wanted to be happy for him, but I knew how things could change quickly when one returned to their element.

"You did not." I smiled and grasped his hand. "We should clean up."

"Are you still upset?" My skin had grown darker as I sank into my sadness. Our time with Mateo was ending, as I knew it would. Yet, I was sad; how could I not be?

I did not lie. I would not lie to Mateo. Instead, I left him in bed and went to the bathroom. The worm was not convinced that we would be left behind.

"You'll see, Quinn. Our treasure will not forsake us. Not now." I did not tell Helmin that it was being naïve. It knew how I felt.

Mateo joined us In the shower, and I gave him a half-hearted smile as we cleaned up. His kisses were still in earnest. My skin was still a shade of cerulean. Once we were clean, we put on robes, and I retrieved my dinner from the pass-through hatch.

"Were fae always vegetarians?" Mateo asked. This was the second night he'd seen me eat. My diet mainly comprised greens, vegetables, fruits, and legumes. Though I liked to add cheese and eggs from time to time. Tonight's dinner was roasted root vegetables and tofu with a balsamic vinaigrette.

"While most of us are agrarian, a few groups hunt small game. I've sustained myself without that protein source." My skin color slowly returned to its neutral pink-gray tone as Mateo continued to ask questions. They were about my favorite foods, favorite places, and what books I enjoyed reading. I answered them to distract myself.

As I finished dinner, Mateo brought out the spiced whiskey. He offered me a glass, but I declined. I did not want to be tempted back into his bed. I would find no comfort in it now. Even knowing that, I could not bring myself to leave him.

The decision was eventually made for me when we heard a gentle knock around five in the morning.

"Yes?" Mateo asked.

A soft, feminine voice called out, "Love, it's us."

Mateo threw the door open. His companions stood at the entrance with a bag in each hand. He gasped and cried as he tugged them into the room. While he'd been distracted, I dressed in my shirt and slacks from the previous evening.

"Quinn." He turned to face me as his companions followed. I had seen them before, but we'd never met properly. The surprise on his face as he noticed I had dressed was not lost on me. "I think you've talked to them briefly, but I want to introduce you properly. These are my companions, Mariah and Cyril."

Mariah was a beautiful woman with brown skin, brown eyes, natural black hair, and a dancer's physique. I did not have a hard time imagining her as the lead dancer of a ballet troupe. Or in Mateo's bed. Cyril had dark brown hair and light brown skin similar to Mateo's, though it was a richer hue likely due to his exposure to sunlight. His blue eyes were striking, and I found myself unable to look him in the eye, though he was the shortest individual in the room.

"Did you keep him company all this time?" Mariah asked.

"It was no trouble," I said with a slight nod. Mateo frowned. "Let me leave to let you catch up with each other. I have other things to attend to this morning."

Cyril caught my hand on my way through the door. He pressed a sliver of silver into my palm. "For our gratitude." He was sincere about it. They had no idea what had transpired, and Mateo seemed to be at a loss for words. I took the silver with a nod and left. I did not wait for the door to be shut in my face.

Three Days Later

I lay in my bed, staring at the ceiling, and wondered how I had become so attached to someone who hadn't been more than an acquaintance a short time before.

The door to my residence opened, and then someone shut it behind them. Considering all the locks were keyed to an individual's biometrics, it had to be a manager override that let someone into my bungalow.

"Oh, good, you have not expired."

I glanced at the doorway, and Felven moved further into my bedroom and pressed a button to adjust the opaqueness of the windows to allow light to stream in. I hated it, and yet was drawn to it.

Their tentacles sifted through clothing and other things that I had strewn about the place.

"If I wanted maid service, I would have called for it."

"Funny enough, the service stopped by, and they said you would not let them in for the scheduled cleaning." The tilt of their head and the sharp tone in their song was meant to convey their disappointment. "I came to see if you were ready to return to work, and I also wanted to deliver this."

Felven held out a letter. Paper was rare and expensive. Most used electronic communication of some kind, but I had shut off my cell once I'd returned to my room. The elegant envelope had my name beautifully written across the surface.

"It's from him, isn't it?"

"Yes."

"I don't want it."

"I am not your message service either, Quinn. Take the letter." I took it from their outstretched tentacle, then promptly wadded it up and tossed it into the waste receptacle near my bed.

Felven sighed. "Your clients are asking for you. The spa would like to know when you plan to return to work, and your coworkers are concerned about you."

"You didn't report me to management?"

"Whyever would I do that?"

"Because of Mateo."

Felven leveled a look at me. "You are not the first to become entangled with a guest, nor will you be the last. Though I have to admit, I'm surprised you did after a decade of working here."

"Have you ever dallied with a guest?"

"Once," Felven admitted. "They were here, hiding from relatives. They stayed for quite some time, but once they reconciled, they left, and we never spoke again."

"That's awful, Felven."

"It is the nature of the place in which we live and work. The rules are there for a reason. Anyone who has been here long enough has broken them at least once." Felven sat down on the foot of the bed, their tentacles splayed out across the bedclothes. "But we continue on. Acknowledge the mistake and move forward." They sighed. "All this to say, it will be alright soon enough. Trust your routine, and things will correct themselves."

My routine, the sole reason I did things some days, had remained quiet. It seemed Helmin was as broken as me. I half wondered why its hunger hadn't woken me, but my emotions were so dark, it likely was enough to feed it and pull me into sleep. If Felven had been less of a friend, the cleaning service might have found my corpse with Helmin burrowed halfway through me.

"I can not eat you."

"It is your very nature to eat," I mumbled to the worm, forgetting Felven was in my room.

"Not blindly or mindlessly. Not anymore."

"Quinn?" Felven shook me gently with a tentacle. "You were mumbling. Are you sure you do not need medical attention?" The concern in their tones touched me. I patted their tentacle and sat up. The bedclothes pooled in my lap. Felven vibrated with anxiety. It took everything I had not to reach out and take it from them. "You have a parasite, Quinn."

"Yes." It was careless of me. Or maybe, with my newfound loss, I was also done hiding Helmin.

"The charms and your aura make so much sense now. You have no idea how many have gossiped about you. Some assumed you were an ancient that could curse them out of existence, and the charms were to hide your true visage."

I looked at Felven as the words slowly entered my mind. I felt a smile form on my face, then a grin, until I burst into laughter that quickly turned hysterical. I finally replied as I wiped tears from my eyes. "Oh goddess, if only that were the case. I'm only halfway into my second century!"

Felven's dark orbs seemed to twinkle while their face stayed passive, arranged in the calming smile that everyone always saw. "You are very private. Aloof even. Helpful, but aloof. It is one thing to be that way with guests, but quite another to be distant from those you live and work with."

"I . . . that wasn't my intent. Honestly, I don't know what my intent was. I assumed I was off-putting."

"Did you ever ask?"

I shook my head, ashamed that I had never sought their company or trusted anyone with my private life. A tentacle reached out, caressed my face, then prompted me to lift my head until my gaze met Felven's.

"No time like the present, my friend. The season-end party is on Friday. You should go."

"Will you come with me?" I sounded like a heartbroken adolescent, but I didn't care.

Felven hummed, "Yes. I'll attend with you. If you allow me to select your attire."

"Fine." I smiled at them and got myself out of bed. "I'll let the responsible parties know that I'll return to work tomorrow." Felven remained seated on my bed. Their tentacles roamed about the bedding.

"Thank you, Felven." The humming noise grew louder. "Is there anything else?"

"You are nude." Felven never struck me as anyone who cared much about clothing. Their own wasn't much more than a long jacket.

"I am. I usually sleep naked. Is that a problem?"

"No." Felven seemed to stare, though I couldn't be sure. "Are you planning to shower?"

"Yes." This line of questions was odd. "Why?"

"Would you like assistance?"

"Why would I need assistance?" I gathered a towel from the hook near my bathroom door.

Felven pushed up from the bed and rotated their tentacles to balance their stance. "Maybe assistance was not the correct word. Would you like companionship?"

"Are you offering . . ." My skin shaded to a bright yellow, then shifted to a deep red.

"I am curious. They have interesting appendages. Tell them my name."

"The worm's name is Helmin. It is interested in you, and so am I. Please." I inhaled, invigorated by my newfound freedom, "Join us."

Felven began to remove their jacket as I turned toward the bathroom to start my shower. To say that the next ninety minutes were enjoyable would be an understatement.

Six Months Later

A call came in from the front desk to my phone. I smiled at it. Though Felven usually called with their personal number if they wanted to talk, chatting with them always put me in a better mood.

Felven and I developed a better friendship, and through that, I've learned to be more open with individuals around me. They introduced me to others, and I've discovered that Helmin was not the detractor I once thought it to be, despite my family's insistence. Even other fae were less intimidated once they learned of my circumstances.

"Hello?"

"Ah, excellent. You are still awake."

"You know that this is my reading time. Is the front desk so boring this evening?"

"Not precisely." Felven paused, which wasn't like them.

"Has your vocalizer malfunctioned?"

"No. It has not," Felven said with playful annoyance in their tones. "You were requested by a guest."

"Oh? And that warranted a call? You have my schedule."

"Quinn, it's Mateo. He's requested a session with you tomorrow evening."

My heart raced. Helmin was anxious and annoyed in turns. The odd, non-verbal noises it made broke me out of my silence. "That's fine."

"Are you sure? You have the right to refuse."

"I'm sure. Please book the rooftop meditation garden for the session."

"As you wish." Their tone wasn't strictly neutral about it, but I knew they would trust me with what I thought was best.

"And Felven," they made a soft tone in response. "Thank you for calling me. I'll find you afterward and let you know how it went."

"Whatever you do, don't throw him off the roof. That's too many forms to fill out."

I laughed, but I knew Felven was somewhat serious. "Good night, my friend."

"Be well, Quinn."

The following evening, I was already in the garden when Mateo arrived. He was dressed in loose-fitting clothing, which was usual for our meditation sessions. I wore linen slacks and nothing else.

His gaze roamed my body. Helmin did not call him by the pet name it once had for him. *"We will feed, then be done, yes?"*

"Yes, then we'll be done."

"Good."

I smiled as Mateo sat. "Let's begin, shall we? Deep breath." I inhaled.

"Really? After all this time, not a hello or otherwise. I'd even take a 'fuck you,' if you were capable of it. Are you capable of it?"

"And exhale." I let out the breath I held and didn't satisfy his annoyance or curiosity.

"I called, I left messages, I even sent a note."

It was clear he was in distress. Which was good because Helmin could feed. But I held back. My gaze met Mateo's. His dark brown eyes were pools of sorrow. I had thought once that they might have held more, but if that had been the case, things would have turned out differently.

"You didn't stop them, Mateo."

"What?"

"You, in your haste to return to your companions, said nothing. You didn't stop them. I was even paid in silver for my trouble."

Mateo was quiet for a time. I closed my eyes and drew from his ample life force. He had fed quite a lot on someone before meeting me. Which was good because I was angry.

"I kept my promise, Quinn."

"You did. And I release you from it." I opened my eyes, and my skin was a grayish blue, slowly turning to something darker. "I no longer need to hide myself or my abilities."

"I see that." He was quiet for a few more moments. "How is Helmin?"

I took another breath. "Helmin is well." My frustration grew. "If you are not here to meditate, then maybe we should reschedule." I levered to my body out of the cross-legged position I was in while Mateo fumbled about, trying to gain his feet. I headed for the access door when he called out.

"Quinn, wait. Please."

I turned back. "What could you possibly say to either of us that would change anything?"

"I'll wait for you, both of you. I'll wait." He sighed. "I found the protection of a coven close by, not more than thirty minutes from the resort. I've a home there, and I explained things to Mariah and Cy. They didn't know. Please don't blame them. You were right. I didn't say anything."

He stepped closer, and I wasn't sure how close I wanted to be with him again. "Remember when you told me you would give me anything if I removed the compulsion?"

Mateo stopped a few steps from me. "Yes." His eyes lit up with hope, and I nearly caved. Helmin did not.

"He can wait. There are other treasures."

"Whatever you both want. Please, Quinn, Helmin."

"Fifty years."

"What?"

"You can wait for our touch, our affection, our blood, for fifty years from today. If you return at that time and ask us for a relationship, we'll consider your request." I turned back toward the exit. Mateo did not say a word as we left.

One Year Later

"Enter." I called out as the door chime sounded.

I knew Felven would have all the food and drinks, along with anything else they decided to bring with them. They were horribly picky about seating and snacks, but they didn't mind playing games or watching movies. The rest of our small group of permanent workers crowded around my holo display.

Instead of being greeted with tentacles laden with food, I had a large bouquet of paper flowers shoved in my face. "This came for you today," Felven said. They sounded annoyed as I looked for a spot to put the massive display, and Felven looked for a place to put everything else they were holding.

"Dining table." I offered as I put the bouquet on the nearby desk. I looked for a message and found it buried among the flowers. It was artfully rolled up, but I recognized the elegant handwriting of the note.

Quinn & Helmin,
I wish you both my utmost affection and joy.
Your Treasure,
Mateo

"What's all this?" Freddie asked as she snatched the note out of my hand. Her partner, Eilidh, shortly followed, interested in what Freddie was reading. Felven made some kind of noise of dismissal and went to the holo.

"Are you and Helmin dating this Mateo?" Eilidh asked.

"No, not exactly. Why do you ask?" It's not as if I'd left Mateo completely without remedy. We still had his meditation sessions and maintained our professional relationship. Helmin and I might be undecided about a relationship with the vampire, but we were not cruel.

"Paper is a first-anniversary gift," Freddie said with a smile to Eilidh, then kissed her cheek. "Though the bouquet only having forty-nine flowers is odd. Does that mean anything?"

"Maybe. Maybe not. We'll have to wait and see."

"Yes. We will wait and see."

MISCELLANEOUS

Author's Note

Miscellaneous

These are short stories that reside within the Mythical Desires Universe and extend parts of the world building or lore within the universe. These were fun one-off pieces written mostly as initial story ideas that led to other ideas.

All Saint's Day was a short story originally submitted to Armadillo Writer's Workshop. It was meant to be a preface for a longer story, but instead it inspired *Dr. Mason Only Dies At Night* (previously *Death Warmed Over*).

A Toad's Kiss was written when I was toying with the idea of fairytale formats. It inspired some of the prose and direction for *Prince's Tide*.

Content Warnings for All Saint's Day: *on-page sex, blood, teratophilia, necrophilia, emotional manipulation, death of a partner*

ALL SAINT'S DAY

I woke with a fleeting feeling that I had been somewhere else. Like a dream on the edge of my mind, clinging like a spiderweb in a corner. I was warm and loved, unlike now, chilled to the bone and shivering under the covers of my bed. I reached out and found the space next to me empty.

When I heard the toilet flush, I sighed with relief. Clayton had stayed the night, which made me smile to myself. We'd only been together a short time, less than a year, though we've known each other longer. He was a resident doctor at the local Saint's hospital, and I had met him last year when one of his friends brought him to my Halloween party.

My parties were things of legend for the local neighborhood and the college graduate crowd I ran with. Themed decorations were a must, and last year it was all about ghosts. From the illusion spells cast to the beverages and snacks, I looked forward to coming up with a new theme every year. The night I met Clayton, he drank very little, but was amused by my fake ghosts and screaming cats, courtesy of spells I'd learned from a friend.

Summer witches were much better at keeping blossoms growing and plant yields high for fall harvests. Though sometimes you could learn other things if you had a mentor. Magic was flexible like that. The whole trick to it was being in tune with your magic, whatever form it took.

Though after last night's party, I didn't feel very in tune with anything at the moment. It was another great gathering with friends. Clayton rarely stayed the night because of his residency schedule, but last night he had waited out all the guests, kissed me pretty thoroughly and tucked us into bed together. We had talked about moving in together, but hadn't taken the leap yet. He liked his routine, so I took this shift in his normal habits as a sign. Something you get used to being around witches. A lot of things were signs to us.

The first time we spoke, after a quick introduction by our mutual friend, he asked me if I knew the difference between ghosts and zombies. Any witch worth her salt knew. "Ghosts couldn't really be controlled; zombies could," I had said. Though they were both collections of fragmented memories. That's the part people often forget. Memories held a lot of power, and if you could harness them, you could make magic happen.

Footsteps echoed on the wooden floors of my bedroom as Clayton came back and climbed into my bed. I turned towards him and wrapped my chilly hands around his warm body while I hooked my leg around his waist. He was a large man with black hair shaved down and styled, a goatee to match, brown eyes, and well-defined features wrapped in dark brown skin. My pale skin glowed in contrast to his.

"For a minute, I thought you'd left," I whispered.

Clayton reached up and brushed a strand of my long brown hair out of my face. "Never."

That one word statement was odd from a man I knew to be very independent and liked his space. I frowned, unable to think of a reply. He smiled and traced my cheek with his fingers, and kissed my forehead as he held me tight.

Maybe I was coming down with something. Everything seemed a bit off. I tried to figure it out until Clayton's large hand caressed my back, sending warmth along my spine with his magic. Something he's done a few times that always made me feel better.

"You're warm," I murmured. The soft rumble of Clayton's baritone laughter sent a pleasant vibration through me as I drifted in the bubble of comfort he had created. We stayed that way for a few long moments until Clayton rolled away from me and got out of bed.

"Where are you going? You just came back." At least, I think he did. Had we drifted off? I couldn't seem to remember.

"Shower. Wanna join me?"

The blankets went over my head as a reply. He laughed, and the sound caressed my insides like soft fur.

"Suit yourself."

I listened as I heard the shower start and Clayton hum to some nameless tune. As if he were the piper, the soft resonating hum lured me out of bed with a smile as I wandered toward the bathroom to find exactly what my mind conjured. Clayton opened the shower door and beckoned me inside.

"Would you like a hand?" he asked. As my fingers caressed his, warmth seeped into my skin with every inch he explored. My skin reddened from his gentle attention, and I smiled shyly, as if he'd never touched me this way before. Plops of skin and dried blood fell away as he applied a washcloth to my body, wiping away the zombie makeup from the previous night's party.

A bottle opened behind me, and cool liquid flowed onto my head, followed by Clayton's broad hands as he lathered my hair. I never liked strong scents, and this one was overwhelming. Had I picked that? I couldn't remember and tried to ignore the smell as his fingers drifted and massaged my scalp. They only stopped when he gently untangled the knotted mess I had made of my hair with a massive amount of gel I used to create the look for my costume.

Pro-tip: never use magic products for your hair. They never last, and if they interact with other magic, well, let's just say the consequences weren't worth it for me.

"Next year, we need better costumes. I don't think anyone was amused that you were yourself and I was your reanimated corpse girlfriend."

Clayton paused for a moment. I took his silence to mean that he wouldn't argue about it. I was the one who liked parties. He only showed up the first time because he wanted to meet me, so his friend had said.

"I mean, I know you avoided dressing up, but next year, we'll do something fun, like wallflowers, or maybe bees, or cheese dip." I blamed the lack of caffeine on that last bright idea.

His laughter echoed off the tiles. "Cheese dip?"

"We're together now. And as the hosts, we have to come up with something more creative. So no slacking next year, got it?"

"Whatever makes you happy, my Liv," he said as he kissed the top of my head, then turned to shut off the shower. That small joke warmed my heart. Liv was short for Olivia, but he rarely called me by my full name.

Clayton opened the shower door, and the steam followed him out into the bathroom. When I stepped out onto the cold bathroom tiles, I shivered. Clayton came to my rescue and wrapped me in a towel, then took down another to dry my limbs.

"I can do that myself, you know."

"I know." He gave me a gentle smile. "But I want to." He leaned in, kissed me once, then lingered near my lips in a quiet offer of more. When I moved to reciprocate, he pulled away. Only after I gave him a pout did he offer another kiss. "We should get moving. I have a lot planned for today." He wrapped the towel he was holding around his waist and left me in the bathroom.

"Like what? We have an entire apartment to clean up." I followed. It wasn't going to be that hard. Spells would take care of a lot, but even that took an hour or so to whip up.

Clayton went for the dresser drawer, where he kept his clothes, and I headed for my closet. Before I could even open it, he moved behind me and wrapped his arms around my waist, and kissed my ear.

"You're pretty snuggly today." I turned my head to see his face, but he drew me in tighter. His body heat soothed the aches I felt in my bones that even the hot shower hadn't penetrated.

"Just happy you're here."

"Oh, where else would I be?" I ran my hands along his well-muscled forearms.

"Wanna do me a favor?"

The change in subject was noted, but I let it go. Clayton rarely asked for favors. "Like what?"

"Wear my favorite outfit?" He slowly turned us so that I would see the outfit laid out on the dresser.

"Do I have to?" I frowned at the summer dress. It was November. It was only luck that we lived in Texas, and it wasn't terribly cold, though my body tried to tell me otherwise as I shivered slightly. Clay must have felt it because he rubbed my arms in response.

"It's a special day, and I want it to be perfect." We stood like that for a few more minutes as my body responded to Clayton's warmth, and my shivers dissipated.

"Okay, if you insist. Weirdo." I turned and poked at his chest as I wiggled out of his arms. Clayton caught my hand as my towel dropped to the floor. In retaliation, I pulled his towel off too. We stood naked, pressed together, and I sighed against his comforting form.

"I missed you." The words were so soft I almost didn't hear them.

"Two steps in the opposite direction, and you missed me?" I looked up at him. "You'll have to let go sometime if you want me to wear clothes." He smiled, but the playfulness I loved so much didn't reach his eyes. He distracted me from my concern as he caressed my face and tried to tame the same stubborn strands of hair.

"I know, I'm being weird." He kissed me, then released me with a gentle push for good measure.

A slight chuckle escaped me as I walked over to the dresser. I noticed an addition to his favorite outfit. "Seriously? You want me to wear these?" I held up the g-string lace panties from one finger. "These are bedroom panties. They don't leave the house."

"Today, and today only, those leave the house. I have plans for those later." He plucked them from my finger, then held them out for me to step into. His beautiful umber face and his brown eyes held the kind of passion that I fell into when I first met him. We teased each other a lot, and today was no different. If he could make plans, I could make plans too.

I stepped into the panties. Clayton slipped them up my legs and fit them around my waist. He even adjusted the string in the back. My heart raced as his hands slipped over my ass, up my back, over my shoulders, and down my arms. The gentle touch gave me warm gooseflesh.

Fuck, okay, maybe he was better at the long game than I was. I leaned forward and stole another kiss. A longer one this time, telegraphing my intent as I ran a hand down the front of him and stopped just short of his groin.

"Plans. Plans," Clayton chanted as if to remind himself and put a little distance between us. "You're distracting in the best way, but plans . . . okay?"

"I have a different plan. You, me, a box of condoms . . . or two."

"Okay, that plan has merit," he said with a smirk, and the look in his eyes lit me up from the inside out. "But I'm hungry, and I'm sure you're hungry. So let's say we go for a bite to eat, and if you want to come back and do your plan, I could be persuaded." He leaned in to kiss me, then kissed me again.

I was delighted with the idea of us in all the various positions and places. Then my stomach grumbled, which made us laugh. "Okay, definitely food first. Then we figure out what to do next."

"Agreed. I'll let you finish," Clayton said as he went back to pulling clothes out for himself.

"Okay." I put on the bra that matched the g-string, then put on the blue summer dress. Clayton liked it because it matched my eyes. He had picked out my favorite ankle socks and sneakers, too. So, it wasn't entirely his outfit. He liked heels. I'd worn them often enough to events and to bed for him that I knew which ones were his favorites. I hated heels and wore tennis shoes or sandals if I had a choice.

Clayton dressed in a navy v-neck T-shirt and dark jeans while I watched. As he was putting on his socks and chucks, I imagined peeling all of it off him as soon as he was finished.

Instead, I behaved and went to the living room to see what I could clean up before we left. I stopped dead in my tracks as I remembered what it looked like the night before. We had promised each other that we'd pick it up in the morning. My living room had been a mess of party favors, discarded beverage containers, candy wrappers, and green vapor.

What I found was nothing. Not only a lack of trash, but absolutely nothing. No furniture, decorations, or family pictures. The room was bare. I screamed.

"Olivia! What's wrong?" Clayton came up behind me, and I turned to meet him.

"I've been robbed. Everything is gone, Clay. Even the trash! Who the fuck takes trash!?"

"Calm down. There's a logical explanation, I promise."

"Well, I'd like to know what the fuck it is. My living room is empty!"

"Remember that gag the Harris brothers pulled, the one you told me about?"

I remembered it. The Harris brothers had made everything invisible or phased it out of the physical dimension. They promised never to pull that again. "Did they fucking do this after they promised?"

"They were here last night." Clayton's face was blank for a moment, then sympathy materialized on his face. I didn't know if it was for me or for the Harris brothers.

"I'm going to shove my foot so far up their asses they'll be growing leaves out of their ears!" I marched to the coat closet and slammed it open. A growl escaped my lips as I realized the only garment left inside was my jean jacket. Somehow they managed to empty everything else out of that too! I yanked it out and slid it on. "Ugh! I'm going to turn them green for good measure!"

I went for the door, and Clayton stopped me. "Hey, hold up. I know you're pissed, but they probably got wasted and are at home sleeping it off. Think we could hold off on green vengeance for one day?" He held up a forefinger in my face as a plea and a rebuke. I slapped it out of the way.

"I'm going to turn them into shrubs! I don't care how drunk they are. My things are gone!"

"I know, I know." Clayton offered a hug, and I went to him willingly. "Just for today. Let's grab some food before your stomach eats itself, then enjoy the rest of the day. Tomorrow we can turn the Harris brothers into topiaries." He rubbed along my back, and I felt my anger slip away like mist. "Feel better?"

I sighed. "Yes. Okay. Today, food. Tomorrow, chase down the Harris brothers."

"At least you don't have to clean up after the party."

"You have a point." I sighed, temporarily defeated, and he laughed. This time I saw playfulness light up his eyes, and that sent a shiver of happiness through me. He offered his hand, and I took it as he led me out the door.

The walk to the cafe Clayton and I enjoyed was nice, but odd. Buildings seemed older. People walked by whom I didn't recognize. The neighborhood seemed odd. Or it felt strange, as if it had changed while I wasn't paying attention. I couldn't quite put my finger on it.

When our server showed up, I realized I didn't recognize her. "Hi Tracy," I read her name tag. "Are you new here?"

Tracy shook her head and was about to answer when Clayton interrupted. "She doesn't want to talk about that, honey. She's here to take our order. Right?" Clayton looked up at her, and Tracy shrugged and nodded.

We gave our order, Tracy left, and I had a bone to pick. "What's wrong with you? I've never seen you be that rude to anyone, ever? Why did you do that?"

"I'm sorry. You're right. I'll apologize." He got up and went to talk with Tracy. I watched as he spoke, and Tracy's eyes widened a little, then she nodded. Clay nodded and then turned to come back to our table. "There, all better. I let my hunger get the best of me."

"Your mother would have had your ass for doing something like that."

"I know. Don't tell on me, okay?" He gave me a small smirk before he reached his hand out across the table to take mine.

He seemed nervous but relaxed again as Tracy returned with our coffee. She smiled at me with kind but sad eyes. I wasn't sure why that was, but I let it go. A tip wouldn't make up for Clayton being rude, but at least it would make me feel a little better. I sipped my coffee and felt the hot fluid move through me like lava down a mountain.

Our food showed up, and it smelled wonderful. Frankly, I was so hungry it could have been a plate of garbage, and I could have eaten it if it smelled this good. The flavors, the smells, were all so delicious. I shoved eggs and bacon into my face while I saw Clayton take three bites of toast and a sip of his coffee. "What's got you so sour-faced?"

"Tired is all," Clayton said. He seemed closed off, distant compared to this morning. I wondered what had him worried.

"Oh? I could fix that, you know. I know a guy who knows a lady who gives amazing blow jobs," I said in a conspiratorial whisper across the table.

"Do you now? I should get their number," he said, chuckling as he took another sip.

"Great service, curbside even. Delivery with a smile, ten minutes or less."

Clayton tried not to laugh as he took a sip of his coffee, choked, then laughed anyway as he held his nose. "That's a new one." His face betrayed his amusement as he cleared his throat.

"Oh, you liked that, huh? I got more." I grinned as I ate another bite of hash browns, and he finally smiled back.

"Of that, I have no doubt."

We finished breakfast and headed for the park across the street. The weirdest déjà vu hit me as we walked together. I knew this was our favorite walk, but it had the feel of memory instead of treading a well-worn path.

"Do we have time in your plans to visit the shelter today?" It was only a little further up the path. There were some places that took in everyone, four legs and humanoid alike. The wards and building structure were created in such a way as to maintain multiple species, considering all the different kinds of magic. The shelter near my apartment was older and could only handle small species of magic, which meant that they mostly took in domesticated animals and familiars.

We'd often talk about finding a pet or familiar that liked us both, raising kids, and buying a house. I realized that's what was suspiciously missing this morning on our walk.

"Sure, we have time."

It was practically dead when we entered the shelter, which wasn't surprising the day after Halloween. The attendant pointed us toward the dog runs, and we walked up and down the rows, admiring the dogs. All of them seemed to back away from me or growl when I got close. I frowned, and so did Clayton. Animals never had a problem with either of us, so their response to me was alarming.

The whines and barks grew more intense as we moved through the rows. When I tried to speak calmly to one, it lunged at me. Clayton caught me, so I didn't do a face-plant in my effort to scramble back from the door.

"I don't get it. Do I smell bad or something?" I gave myself an exploratory sniff. All I could smell was the flowery shampoo.

"Dogs are sensitive to all kinds of things. Maybe something is bothering them we can't see," Clayton offered. The growling and barking grew louder.

I shivered as the barking escalated. "I grew up with animals and I've never had a problem before. Maybe I could do a quick calming spell." I lifted my hand, and Clayton grabbed it.

"We don't know what's affecting them. We shouldn't add to it. Besides, we don't work here. We can tell the attendant on the way out."

"But I wanted to stay longer." I sighed as I lowered my hand, still confused as to why most of the animals near us were so scared or on alert.

"I know. Love, I know." He kissed the top of my head, trying to placate me. I wrapped my arms around him as his arm wrapped around my shoulders.

We were about to leave when I noticed a dog near the entrance. As he stood at the door to his run, with his tongue out and half a grin on his face, his green eyes captured my attention. I let go of Clayton and walked over to the door. He didn't respond like the others as I approached. I reached my hand up to the gate, and he licked it. I looked up at the name tag and smiled. It said, "Bruce."

Bruce was about 80 pounds of mutt and muscle. When Clayton came over, he was still calm and eager, sniffing our hands as we held them out. Bruce's fascinating green eyes were even more striking up close. Every animal has intelligence and sentient thoughts, though familiars had another level to them that allowed for better communication with humanoid species.

I couldn't immediately tell if he was a familiar, but his eyes made me wonder.

Familiars were allowed their own spaces with very few restrictions. Domestics were often kept separate from each other to minimize their instincts being triggered.

When Bruce made a loud bark, our section of the shelter went quiet. Moments passed before a few soft whines could be heard, and the smell of urine drifted down the row. I looked at Bruce with a bit of surprise, but he only stood there with his mouth open and tongue hanging out as I looked into his piercing green eyes.

"Wow, Bruce, that was impressive." I turned to Clayton. He was glancing around the shelter with curiosity written on his face. "What do you think, babe? Can we help him?" I asked.

"I don't know. He's pretty big."

Bruce made a half-whine, half question-like noise, and I was in love.

"Oh my god, would you look at him? He's perfect, Clay." I was not giving up on the idea that Bruce was coming home with us. I watched as Clayton rocked on his feet with apparent indecision. I bit my lip and waited, but was hopeful, too. I hoped he would see this as our next step.

"Okay, okay. Let's go fill out the paperwork," Clayton sighed. I hopped up from the floor, reached for his hand, and pulled him along with me toward the adoption station.

"We'll be right back, Bruce!" There was a quick yip in response. "You won't regret this, babe! Besides, it's good practice. You know, for our future." I said as I marched forward, but he stopped instead. I heard him take a deep breath, and I turned to look at him and saw tears streaking down his face.

"What's wrong? If it's too much, I understand—" I worried that I'd pushed Clayton too far. We'd talked about kids, but our families were at odds a lot and were trying to let them adjust to us being together. We both came from very traditional magic disciplines that didn't always see eye to eye on things.

"No, no, it's not that at all." He sighed. "I. . . I love you," he said with a barely audible voice. I watched as tears emerged and spilled down his face. It disturbed me. I'd only seen Clayton cry when his grandfather passed. They had been close, but this seemed like something more.

"Hey, hey. It's okay. I love you too. I'm sorry I'm demanding. We don't have to do this. I like Bruce. Maybe we can take a few days to decide," I offered.

"No, nope." He sniffed and wiped his face. "We'll get Bruce outta here. He can go with us." He hugged me tighter and then walked us toward the door that led back to the front desk.

"With us, where?"

Clayton smiled and tugged me toward the adoption desk. "You'll see."

Bruce was possibly a half-familiar. The shelter staff weren't surprised, considering what we witnessed. As a pittie mix with brilliant green eyes, light brown fur on his back and legs, with white fur on his tummy and paws, he was very distinct.

After we adopted him, we walked back to my apartment. Clayton directed me toward his vehicle, where I found a picnic basket waiting in the back. Bruce immediately hopped in and hung his head out of the vehicle window as we drove off, tongue flying along as we drove down a country road toward a spot Clayton and I knew well.

I grew up around here, and there were little hidden gems all over the place. Immense fields. Splendid views. The first time I brought Clayton to what we would later call our spot, he was flabbergasted. City boy that he was, he had no idea what he'd been missing.

We pulled into a deadend with a trail that led off into a field with a perfect hill for watching the sunset. Bruce ran ahead of us. Clayton grabbed the picnic basket, and we walked hand in hand, enjoying the bright, warm afternoon.

"This is a pleasant surprise." I meant it. It had been a few months since we'd visited our favorite picnic spot. We both liked it because the spot was always a lush green with soft grass, and close to the hilltop was a small cemetery with family plots. It was a case where our natural magics co-existed.

"Good." He lifted my hand to his lips to kiss. "I'm glad you approve."

The sun was still pretty high in the sky when we made it to our spot, and Bruce ran for all it was worth. He returned to check on us every once in a while, but mostly he ran down whatever he could chase to his heart's content. My heart was content, too.

Clayton poured us glasses of wine and pulled out a fruit and meat platter, which wasn't nearly enough, I thought, but that was okay. I wasn't hungry at the moment. Well, not for food, anyway. We watched Bruce and drank our wine. About halfway through my second glass, I leaned over and kissed Clayton. As he returned it with unchecked intensity, we discarded our wine glasses and fell back on the picnic blanket. Focused on each other as we continued to kiss and caress all the places we knew so well.

It was everything I had wanted as Clayton's hands drifted along my thighs, and I worked to undo his jeans and open his fly. I leaned over him and reached a hand down his pants as we kissed. He wasn't wearing his boxers, and I moaned into his mouth.

"You like that, huh?" he asked, half out of breath from our kissing.

"I fucking love it," I said into his mouth as I worked him over with my hand.

"Come here." He put his hands on my waist and tugged on my hips.

I let go of him and moved forward so he could push my panties aside and press his thumb in just the right spot to tease me. I was wet; he didn't have to do much.

"Fuck!" I smacked his chest lightly. He stopped what he was doing, surprised by my response. "Did we bring condoms?"

"No, I didn't remember to grab any. Sorry," Clayton said, sounding a little guilty.

"Shit," I sighed. "Do you want to risk it?"

"Yes. With you. Always."

"God, you're so fucking hot! I love you, Clay."

"I love you too, Liv," he said, but his voice held an edge of sadness.

Well, I wasn't going to have it. Not today. I took Clayton in my hand and guided him inside me. Fuck, his dick was like riding a column of flame that went straight to the core of me. I came within a few minutes as I ground my hips onto his hard-on. He grinned as I caught my breath.

"Hey," I tapped him on the chest, "we're not done yet." I peppered his face with kisses to make my point.

"I wouldn't dream of it," he said with a grin.

I could hear Bruce bark and play, which was comforting as we went at each other. Clayton sat up and kept me on his lap as we rocked our hips slowly. He worked at my sundress, and when my breasts were exposed, and my top was pooled around my waist, he dipped his head to suck and tease one hard nipple after the other. I came again, and my body shook with it.

After that, he behaved like a man on a mission, and before I could register what was happening, I was on my knees as he put himself directly behind me. He tossed the sundress's skirt up and moved my panties again. When he slid home, it was everything I could do to keep a loud moan from escaping my lips. I came again as he played with my clit, and thrust into me.

Eventually, Clayton was above me, and I was on my back as I looked up at him. He kissed my face and ground himself into me as if it was the last fuck he'd ever get. I wrapped my legs around him and rode him for all it was worth. When he finally let go, he buried his head into my breasts, and I could feel his tears mix with our sweat.

"Clayton, sweetie, what's wrong? You've had this weird mood all day. Talk with me."

He looked over his shoulder at the horizon. "The sun is going down. You'll know soon enough," he said as he pulled away from me.

I was stunned for a moment, then my brain processed what he said. Sundown broke enchantments. Spells. What had he done? I turned as Bruce approached us but sat on a far corner of our blanket, where he whined at something. Clayton put himself back together and helped me with my dress. He took my hand as I sat up, and we watched the sun sink into the horizon.

Everything came back. We had been here before. This was where our daughter was conceived. We'd forgotten protection and left it up to fate, which gave us a summer baby. But something went wrong.

I remember Clayton covered in blood as he looked at me, and I held his hand while doctors ran around the room. I knew, even then, I was dying. I was more worried about our daughter. I kept asking him, and he wouldn't answer me while we were in the delivery room, but I wanted an answer now.

"Lily?" I sobbed then and covered my mouth. He reached for me and held me tight as I cried. "What happened to Lily, Clayton?"

"She's with her grandparents today. I know you would have wanted to see her, but I didn't want to risk the magic falling apart too soon. Lily has your eyes and my hair. She's smart, beautiful, and wants to be a doctor like her old man," he said through his own tears. "She's doing really well, Olivia. Even got the family skills. She'll be a really gifted necromancer one day."

"What happened to you, Clayton? How could you do this? The man I knew never wanted to follow in his parent's footsteps." His parents were morticians. The man I knew aspired to be a doctor to save people, not manage their last moments.

"You died," Clayton yelled as he broke down and sobbed more while he held onto me.

"Tell me, Clay. Tell me why." I held him as much for his sake as mine, unwilling to look at him, reluctant to let him go.

"It was so sudden. I was doing a morgue rotation at the time." He didn't pull away from me as he remembered. He shook with grief. "I hid you in the morgue. Created a stasis spell and made sure your parents buried someone that looked like you. A Jane Doe we'd done an intake on a few days before that was close enough that all I needed was a glamour."

"The first time I brought you back was November first. Four months after you died. You remembered the previous year's party like it had happened the night before. It was a perfect day."

He eased up, holding me more gently and giving us space to look at each other. I can only imagine what my face looked like.

He frowned. "I'm sorry, Liv. I'm so sorry I couldn't let go. We had a perfect life, and suddenly it was gone. All I had left of us was our daughter, and it wasn't enough."

"How many times have you brought me back?" I was curious how far Clayton had gone from the path he'd chosen.

"Ten."

"Ten? How is that possible? That would take an extreme amount of life force. More than any person has in a lifetime." Stealing life force was illegal. Even if you gave it freely, there were legal agreements. No council or judicial body would ever have approved using life force to bring someone back unless it was a dire emergency. There was absolutely no way they would ever condone it ten times.

"Corpses always have residual life force. I only took enough from them to build up what I needed. I made sure it wasn't enough to damage the body. As long as no one moved you, and the stasis spell stayed intact, your body acted like a battery until I triggered your reanimation."

"The Harris brothers?" Because if he'd done this ten times, it might explain why my apartment looked so empty.

"They kept their promise." He gave me a sad smile as he wiped his face. "Your parents let me have your place for a few years out of pity. Then they came for your things, and I couldn't stop them. We weren't together long enough. I paid the rent even after my parents helped me out while I was finishing my residency with a house not far from their place."

"Is that where Lily lives?" Clayton nodded.

I didn't know what else to ask. I looked at my hands and noticed the blue-green tinge that often signaled the mortal slide toward death for humans. The magic was fading with the sinking sun. I tried to fathom just how much effort he'd put into this so we could relive the day Lily was conceived. For ten years, he waited for this day, each year, to bring me back. It broke my heart, and I couldn't let it continue. He had to move on.

"Clayton, listen to me. I love you." I reached for his face and held it between my hands as I tried to say all the words that squeezed my heart and tightened up my throat in what I knew were my final moments. "I will always love you. Tell Lily I love her. Tell her all the things a mother would say to her."

He tried to hide his eyes from me through his sobs. "Clayton, look at me. Ten years is enough. You have to move on, for Lily's sake. Please. Please. Please," I kept saying it until he kissed me.

I kissed him back with everything I had, and I could feel myself beginning to fade as the sun went down. I didn't want to leave, but at least I would leave this earth knowing my daughter survived and the love of my life would be there for her.

"It's okay. It's okay, Clayton. I'm okay. Take care of Bruce for me."

Clayton laughed through his tears and nodded. Bruce barked once as the last bit of sun slipped past the horizon. We looked at each other, and I saw him smile one last time before I pushed myself away from him.

"No! Liv, come back, please!" Clayton choked on a sob. "Olivia!" I looked back at him once as he yelled my name before darkness greeted me.

I opened my eyes to the mild shock that I could see anything. For the longest time, I'd only heard voices or music. Being able to see was new.

A young woman was doing something across the room. I recognized it as a workroom that witches often used for magic work. When I looked down, I noticed I could see through my hands. Someone had coalesced my spirit.

"Hi, Mom." The woman smiled at me.

I looked up and knew in my heart who the woman was standing across the room from me. "Lily?"

She nodded.

"Does your father know you summoned me?" I remembered my last moments with Clayton. I didn't want to hurt him like that again.

She shook her head no. "I need your help, and I didn't know who else to ask."

"Whatever you need, darling. How can I help?"

"I need you to translate a spell you wrote that reverses possession."

"Who's possessed?"

"A guy who is holding Dad hostage."

"Shit."

"Yeah."

"Okay, let's get to work." I tried not to pay attention to the fact that my skull was sitting on the counter next to me while I helped my daughter work through my spellbook. I couldn't help but have a smile on my face, though. My beautiful girl was every bit as talented as her father and me.

A TOAD'S KISS

"HA! I say!"

He was indignant the moment that he heard the subject of the story, completely and totally so. And this happened to be a familiar point with Grandpa Ernest. The family was quite used to it, and I doubt my sister would have even brought the story up if she had known that Grandpa Ernest was within hearing distance.

Some just assumed that the old reprobate was out of his mind. It's certainly possible, considering his age. He was much older than anyone had ever known. Lived much longer than was natural, my mother had said, and she had said it out of kindness, since she was Ernest's daughter.

The problem was, you see, about a myth. About a rumor that had gone round and round in these parts, and partially perpetuated by Ernest himself. There are some who say it wasn't old age that affected his memory. No, in truth, it was something seeming much less sinister.

A kiss.

Indeed, as the story goes, a kiss did Grandpa Ernest in, or did something to him. No one is quite sure what. Grandpa used to constantly ramble and would spout off about strange things: about shelters with ice on the sides that you could see through and did not melt, and trees that reached to the sky, filled with this ice he spoke of, and stone. I've never seen them, not in my time. Trees certainly, as birds make homes there, but I've never seen them have many rooms like Grandfather used to speak of, and he hasn't spoken of them for a long while.

Only today did he suddenly make a protest as my sister was telling all the smallings stories. Her collection of tales given by fairies and the like. Or passed on by others, some even made up on her own. Storytelling was an art. My sister had a gift. I could remember times myself when she would sit and spin tales of beasts and fish, animals and fowl. Some of them were monstrous; some very comforting.

Today she was sharing a tale about a human. A young girl who found herself by a pool saw a frog and fell deeply in love with him. She took him home and fed him and kept him in a shoebox, of all things. But he was comfortable, so the story goes, until she kissed him and he turned into a man. Horrid things humans are, and why ever a frog would want to be a man was beyond me, but it was a warning to the children, really, to stay away from humans. Hop away at the first sign. That is, when they finally had legs to hop.

And today, Grandpa caught wind of the story, heard it somehow and came crashing through, knocking dirt about, splashing water and croaking loudly.

"Hogwash!" he exclaimed after his first exclamation. "Whatever it was, whoever that vile thing calling herself a woman was doesn't turn frogs into men. You have it backwards. Look at me, you have it backwards! I was a man once: long hair, two feet, a nose. Now look at me—look at me!" he shouted in his excitement, scaring several who were around listening into stillness as they watched. "I'm a toad! Old and ugly! I'm a toad!"

No one could argue with this, for indeed he was an old toad, not that anyone thought he was ugly. It was just then that Mother came onto the scene and prodded him back towards his own shelter near the pond and away from the shallows.

Mother told me once a story about why Grandpa raves on like he does. I don't know if it was to protect my feelings or to give me something to think about, to make an excuse, as it were. Toads have very sensitive hearts. This is a well-known fact. Grandfather had said some very nasty things and shocked me and my mother. I was nearly heartbroken. But mother explained after he hopped away.

"Son, you mustn't take everything your grandfather says to heart. I know that's hard, but I learned a long time ago it is for the best. I'll tell you in love and honesty, he does not mean what he says. He knows this, but it's hard for him sometimes. And the older he gets, the worse it is. See, your grandpa is right. He wasn't always a toad. Your grandma told me this because she saw it herself. Took care of him after he wandered into the pond and nearly drowned."

She licked at my eyes with her comforting tongue, and I took a deep breath and calmed a little. What Mother was telling me was amazing, mostly because no one really believed Grandpa Ernest. They thought he had taken leave of his senses, with no hint of a common-toad thought left in his brain.

"He fell in love with her right on the spot. His frog heart warmed and calmed with the comfort of the water and companionship. It's the lingering human heart that gives him trouble, I think. Beyond my understanding, certainly. Grandpa says things with such passion, such longing at times, it's easy to see why he misses what he was, and why some young toads end up getting kissed, never to be seen again, and others lucky to come away with their lives."

I keep that in mind when Grandpa rants on about vile women and such. He doesn't mean it. I know that now. But I do wonder sometimes what it would be like to be human. To love as a human does. Maybe someday, when I'm brave enough, I'll venture off and find a human to love me and be kissed. Someday.

IMPORTANT EVENTS IN HISTORY

MAGICAL SPECIES PACT OF 1452

As trade and expansion became more prevalent, territorial wars and colonization became more commonplace. While harvesting parts of magical beings had always been unseemly, the trade and expansion of different empires pushed it into high gear. It was at this point that the Council of Elders, the wisest and oldest magical beings in Europe, came together to create the Magical Species Pact to protect magical beings or anyone who used magic. The pact made magical beings inert or non-magical upon death. If any part of the being was magical, it would render any magic that part or person carried inert. It effectively enforced tolerance between species that shared the same continent.

What they did not understand at the time was how this would affect beings with regenerative powers, such as phoenixes. Magical species that go through a cycle of renewal, such as phoenixes, have a duality of power, as their death generates magic that causes a rebirth, allowing the individual to keep their magical abilities, whatever those were. There's been some side effects attributed to the pact, as phoenixes have reported issues with memory loss since its enactment.

Nor was death magic taken into account. Of the number of elders that were represented by the council, very few had any dominion over the dead or undead. This was the loophole that allowed Joseph Florentine to thrive.

Necromantic War: 1873 to 1878 (the Necro War)

The major theater of war was in Europe and the Prussian Empire, though it spilled over into parts of the Russian Empire as well. Joseph Florentine had been an exceptional necromancer who rose to power in the mid-1800s. His platform centered on allowing magic users the rights and freedoms to use magic as they pleased. He and his followers wanted to abolish the Magical Species Pact created by the Council of Elders to protect magic users. Florentine considered it the height of hubris that one of the most powerful groups of magical beings in Europe had forced magic users on that continent into the pact.

It took many magical species, including necromancers, vampires, and non-magical species (mostly humans) to fight off Florentine's forces.

About the Author

M.L.(Mel) Eaden works by day in the tech industry, but at night, she reads books, writes stories, and is an avid board gamer. Originally from the sunflower state, she migrated to one with a lone star for work and sunshine. She has indie-published several books and short stories from the same queer-centric universe. She's also published several contemporary short stories in anthologies.

There are more great things to find at mleaden.com—blogs, reviews, and her latest newsletter.
Sign up today at mleaden.com and receive a free downloadable short story!

ALSO BY M.L. EADEN

You can find more books from the
Mythical Desires Universe at:
mleaden.com/books

Or sign up for the newsletter:
mleaden.substack.com